SEVEN FOR SCILLY COVE

Kevin Major

To the team at Breakwater Books, many thanks for your continuing support and belief in Sebastian, no matter what turn he takes. To editor Marnie Parsons, thanks so very much for your insight and guidance when it matters most. And to my wonderful, caring family—my heart beats for you all.

For its support, the author wishes to thank ArtsNL, which, last year, invested $5.3 million to foster and promote the creation and enjoyment of the arts for the benefit of all Newfoundlanders and Labradorians.

BREAKWATER BOOKS LIMITED
P.O. BOX 2188, St. John's, NL Canada A1C 6E6
WWW.BREAKWATERBOOKS.COM

LIBRARY AND ARCHIVES CANADA CATALOGUING IN PUBLICATION
Seven for Scilly Cove / Kevin Major.
Major, Kevin, author.
Canadiana (print) 20260217387 | Canadiana (ebook) 20260219177
ISBN 9781778531002 (softcover) | 9781778531019 (epub)
LCGFT: Detective and mystery fiction.| LCGFT: Novels.
LCC PS8576.A523 S48 2026 | DDC C813/.54—dc23
LCC FC2169 .H96 2026 | DDC 709.71809/04—dc23

PAGE LAYOUT: Ian Sullivan Cant

COVER: Tina O'Rourke

THE PUBLISHER GRATEFULLY ACKNOWLEDGES THE SUPPORT of the Canada Council for the Arts; the Government of Canada through the Department of Heritage; and the Government of Newfoundland and Labrador through the Department of Tourism, Culture, Arts and Recreation.

Canada Council for the Arts | Conseil des arts du Canada
Canada
Newfoundland Labrador

PRINTED AND BOUND IN CANADA.

Breakwater Books is committed to choosing papers and materials for our books that help to protect our environment. To this end, this book is made of certified and other controlled material.

FSC www.fsc.org MIX Paper | Supporting responsible forestry FSC® C103567

Well done, you who denounce the sleeveens at work in the world.

It all started with a longish email.

Hi there Sebastian Synard,

I trust you are well and the sun is splitting The Rock(s) today.

I am writing on behalf of KNOT (Keep the Newfoundland Outport Toponyms), of which I am the recently elected president. We are a group of like-minded individuals committed to bringing back the original place names of the Newfoundland communities where we were born and raised and which we still call home.

I, as a prime example, grew up in the outport of Gayside. In 1985, while I was away for training in Massage Therapy, a petition was circulated (I suspect surreptitiously) that resulted in the long-established Gayside being renamed Baytona.

Baytona! I could not believe it. Such an uninspired, insipid name! What were people thinking—that it was going to somehow become the Daytona of the North?

My beloved Gayside had been unceremoniously turfed out, swept into the ash heap of history. All because some hypersensitive residents were ridiculed by a few homophobes from nearby communities.

The adulterated place name was one of the reasons I left Newfoundland, to what I thought was a more broad-minded part of Canada—Toronto. Let's just say it hasn't always lived up to expectations.

Plus all that traffic. To be blunt, I missed the ocean. I missed the serenity of my childhood home. I missed my Gayside.

Three months ago, I retired from my job at the Mississauga Wellness Spa and returned to what I still think of as home. My plan is to open a similar enterprise here in Newfoundland. Similar, but specialized. It will cater in particular to members of the LGBTQ community. I think in that regard it would be unique to the island.

And where to open it? Where else but Gayside (a.k.a. Baytona)!

My enthusiasm is what led me to join KNOT. I was thrilled to find that there was a small but vibrant group of toponymists wanting to see the place names of their home communities revert to what they once were.

Needless to say, we draw our inspiration from the beloved residents of Dildo, Newfoundland, who brought to a screeching halt an intense campaign to change its name. And look where it's landed them. Smack in the centre of international publicity and to the town's name being emblazoned on a hillside, DILDO in letters ten feet high, rivaling those in the hills of HOLLYWOOD. As you well know, Dildo is nothing less than a hotbed of tourism. In midsummer you can hardly get near the place. And (speaking from experience) good luck trying to nab a table at the restaurant of the Dildo Brewing Co. without a reservation.

Do the residents of GAYSIDE (a.k.a. Baytona) realize what opportunity has slipped through their fingers? They should be kicking themselves for their error in judgement. As should be the residents of Famish Gut, Damnable, and Scilly Cove, to name just the hometowns of the KNOT executive.

So, now, to get to the reason for contacting you, Mr. Synard.

In April of next year, KNOT is planning a weekend conference in the inspiring town of Dildo, and nearby Winterton (formerly Scilly Cove), with two guest speakers and multiple thematic sessions. The conference would be open to the public, to be followed by what I'm calling the Grand Tour—a four-day excursion to the aforementioned communities for the executive plus the guest speakers. My request is for you to attend the weekend event to familiarize yourself with our agenda, and then, having arranged accommodation and transportation, shepherd us on the Grand Tour, ending back in Dildo for review and debriefing.

Are you game? KNOT would consider it an honour, given the reputation your tour company has established over the years. We would require a detailed budget of course, but I can safely say you should expect to be well compensated for your efforts.

Yours in toponymy,
Carmel Ann Buttery

ONE: FAMISH GUT

THE EMAIL KNOCKS me sideways. I can hardly believe what I'm reading.

Is Carmel Ann Buttery for real? Is her name even real? It sounds too much of a confection to be plausible.

I search out my copy of *Family Names of the Island of Newfoundland*, and sure enough, there it is in all its glory: "BUTTERY, a surname, of England, from Old French *boterie* - originally a place for storing liquor." No wonder the name had reached Newfoundland by 1722.

Boterie—so much classier than *beverage cabinet*, where I keep my Scotch. I think I might have to rechristen it.

And while I'm in the vicinity of the bookcase, out comes volume two of my *Shorter Oxford*. Several time-honoured steps up from Google. *Toponym, toponymist,* and *toponymy*—they're all there, the study of place names and their derivatives.

Carmel Ann is increasingly for real.

A few years back, I organized a tour for a group of lighthouse fanatics—*pharologists*. A tour that, to say the least, proved a challenge. It left me leery (possibly paranoid) about ever undertaking another customized tour for a group who call themselves something I've never heard of.

Yet "well compensated" is not easily dismissed.

Within limits I can have nerves of steel, if well compensated. Just how well now becomes the question.

I respond to Carmel Ann with a proposed budget, testing the limits of KNOT's largesse. Instead of the seven-seat Dodge Durango that I rented for the lighthouse lot, I propose the twelve-seat Mercedes-Benz Sprinter—roomier, classier, all around more swank. I'm not even positive I can get my hands on one, so the figure is a generous, educated guess.

The accommodation in Dildo is covered by the conference itself. My focus is coming up with four upscale lodgings, in or reasonably near the blandly renamed hometowns of the KNOT executive. Not easily done, given that each must have at least seven ensuite rooms. It takes a lot of googling, yet indeed, they're to be had, and looking rather smart and trendy. I'm getting off on the notion of touring in a style beyond which I am accustomed.

Let's just see what Carmel Ann has to say about my spreadsheet.

In short order, there's but a brief reply. *Two thumbs up. Double your fee and we're good to go. Let me know what I should forward as a retainer.*

Well, if that doesn't blow me out of the water. You can never tell how sizable a bank account lurks behind your average toponymist. I can't wait to meet each and every one of them.

By all accounts—all systems go! What a stroke of good luck. What an unexpected boost to the bottom line. And that bottle of Scotch that's been lingering out of my price range . . . Well, I might just have to move it over to the "distinct possibility" column.

Of course there's a considerable amount of work to do in preparation for the gig, not the least of which is to bone up on the topic of toponymy.

Son Nick, fourth-year university student that he is, offers no help. 'Never heard of it.'

'Welcome to the club.' I give him the Oxford definition. And while I'm at it, those of its derivatives.

'Really. There's a whole field of study devoted to place names?' He takes a sip of Lagavulin before adding 'That must get boring after a while.'

'Not for toponymists, obviously.'

'You mean they go around calling themselves that?'

I remind him he was with me on the lighthouse tour, several days spent hanging out with four grown men who delighted in calling themselves pharologists.

'At least their fixation was tangible. Lighthouses are solid structures—some quite impressive as we saw. Whereas place names are, well, just place names.'

'Not to people who think someone screwed up and made an ungodly blunder by changing the original name. Read this.'

I retrieve the original email and pass the laptop to him. Then sit back, lingering on my own delectable dram until he reaches the end.

'Carmel Ann Buttery? You're not serious? I mean her spa concept might have potential. But KNOT?'

'On the contrary—yes.' The retainer details tell him just how serious.

'This calls for celebration.' I see the wheels turning. In the direction of a meal at one the city's more celebrated restaurants.

'The gig is months down the road. Let's not be counting chickens.'

'From what I hear, Portage does amazing things with poultry. And eggs.'

I take an extended measure of whisky, letting the anticipation intensify.

'I made a reservation already. For tonight.'

'Not!'

'It *is* your twenty-first birthday next week. You'll have grown up. Finally.'

He's smiling broadly. 'In that case, Dom Pérignon.'

'In your dreams.'

'Let's hope the sommelier will have something to fit your budget.'

'I'm thinking Spumante Bambino.'

'I'm thinking K-N-O-T.'

We call it a draw.

I'll miss our verbal jousting when the pest graduates and the time comes for him to move away from home. I've had a taste of it. He spent his first year of university in Halifax, then a semester in Saint-Pierre to do immersive French.

The latter was marred by the tragic end of a personal relationship. It took a heavy toll on Nick. It's taken most of the past year for him to come around to being close to the lad I once knew.

Nick is gay. He's my son—his lifestyle was never going to be an issue, even though I worry about him again encountering the bigotry that's lurking out there, ready to rear its ugly face.

After what happened, he's not been involved with anyone else, as far as I can tell. I don't ask. He tells me what I need to know.

He's secure in who he is. At least it appears so. He has good friends, and that's a huge positive. Still, as a father, I can never *not* worry. All I want for him is what every father wants for his child—to find a purpose in life, to be happy.

For his birthday, his mother (my ex, Samantha) is planning a party for him and his friends at her place, to which I'm invited. In the meantime, Nick and I will eat and drink to his heart's content at Portage, something special for just the two of us.

The divorce happened several years ago, with a custody arrangement that didn't make for smooth sailing. One of the things that firmed up the bond between father and son was hanging out in the kitchen and cooking meals together from scratch. A few disasters, but mostly adventures into recipes that recharged his taste buds and steered him away from prepackaged meals.

All of which has turned him into an excitable young foodie. Fortified by the fact that, every summer since finishing high school, he's worked as a waiter, each successive job taking him higher up the restaurant-rating ladder. Portage is still a few rungs beyond him, which is why he's so keen to step past the entrance on Water Street and be led to our table.

The Portage vibe is innovative, shareable dishes, with emphasis on locally sourced ingredients. Amped up with an uncommon selection of cocktails and wine. Which together has consistently earned it a spot on a list of the one hundred best restaurants in Canada.

We want to go slow and stretch the experience. Nick, I note, is keeping a close eye on the server and how she goes about establishing a rapport with us. Her name is Sabrina. He watches her and the rest of the wait staff as they interact with the cooks across the counter of the open kitchen. When we turn to the menu, he's keen to see how the various dishes have been categorized and described. I suspect he's taking mental notes, thinking how well he might fit in.

'Let me know if you have any questions,' Sabrina says as she pours water for each of us. 'In the meantime, would anyone be interested in a cocktail?'

That we would, given our eyes alight on one intriguingly named Penicillin, made with honey, lemon, ginger, and ten-year-old Laphroaig. Before the glass reaches my lips, I can smell the peat. My anticipation is audible.

'Medicinal,' declares Nick, one step ahead of me, his tasting note one often applied to Laphroaig. 'That explains the Penicillin.'

Clever son orders an appetizer of smoked olives. We're off to a sublime start.

As for the dishes that follow, what's to be said but 'Wow . . . wicked . . . no way . . . ' in praise of focaccia (burrata and hot honey), mussels (ginger and jalapeno), and rutabaga (char siu and apple).

A pause to calm the palate with more Pino Blanc from the Czech Republic. 'Just over a hundred hectares with a winemaking history dating back to Roman times,' the sommelier informs us. 'Typically full sun during the day but cold at night, which means the grapes ripen slowly, giving that clean, full flavour of stone fruit.'

'Apricot definitely,' says Nick, adding, 'Balanced, with a very nice minerality.'

That's my boy—forging past his teenage years with a viticultural vengeance. Impressing the sommelier, whose own youthful enthusiasm means they hit it off from the start.

'Went exceptionally well with the seafood,' I point out. 'And I have my eye on the pork dumplings. What do you think?'

'Absolutely,' says Nick. 'But not the ribeye. Which lets you off the hook.'

He knows my wallet still has boundaries. *'Thrift, thrift, Horatio!'*

He looks back at the menu. Killing time, desperate for a comeback.

'Though this be madness, yet there is method in't.'

Very good.

'I call it budgeting. A very useful life skill.' I'm smirking.

'You're the one who introduced me to Hamlet, remember? On YouTube. I think I was maybe thirteen.'

And a very good deke.

But I do indeed recall that bonding moment, one under particularly tough circumstances. 'David Tennant in a T-shirt. He was brilliant. Shakespeare helped us both a lot that night.'

'A game changer.'

Really?

'As far as leading me into an arts degree.'

Leading *me* to something that's been on my mind for a while. 'What do you figure you'll do after you graduate?'

'I've been thinking about it for a while actually.'

I would like to think of that as an understatement.

'Get a job. Make some money.'

That I like.

'Save up all I can for a year. Then I'd like to travel. I'm thinking Europe.'

News to me. Then again, I shouldn't be surprised.

I've read about young tech fellows who start their own businesses when they're hardly past puberty and make a shit-load of money. That's not Nick obviously. Travel is good. Do it while you're young I say, before you get tied down.

Which is perfectly fine with me. As long as he's enjoying life. And, I would add, paying his own way, as I did at that age. If the truth be told, I envy his plans. It's something I wish I had done before I ended up married.

Should I ask what sort of job he'd be looking for? Probably not. The way he's been soaking up the experience this evening, his aspirations are clearly high.

'Tell you what. I'll give you free rent and board for the year. To help you save.'

'Deal.'

I love it, even if it was rather quick, even if he was expecting it. A win-win situation, especially for his old man.

All of which makes the pork dumplings, the Jerusalem artichokes, and the burger carpaccio (pinch-hitting for the rib-eye) go down wonderfully well. As does the mango pudding topped with bakeapples.

The digestif we save for home. It, of course, is Scotch.

Since he's turned legal, Nick's taste in whisky has refined to the point he's entirely dependent on my *boterie* (a.k.a. *beverage cabinet*) for a dram, not having sufficient funds himself to purchase anything approaching the calibre of what's located there. Before we imbibe, there's generally what Nick has been known to call "spirited debate" about which bottle to bring forth.

It's a scene that I've come to relish, between father and now adult (albeit evolving) son. Sharing what I think of as one of life's greater pleasures. We will keep it to a single but healthy dram for each of us before returning the bottle to where it will again wait patiently with its soulmates.

On this auspicious occasion, however, there is no debate. What little remains of a bottle of Laphroaig 25 Year Old Cask Strength tops by far anything else on offer. (A bottle given to me by a lawyer acquaintance, payment-in-kind for investigative work I undertook for him a few years back.) I have, in fact, been saving this rapturous remnant for this very occasion.

Nick and I each lift a glass to our nose and inhale, letting Laphroaig do what only Laphroaig can do in cask for a quarter-century.

'Brine and iodine'—*of course*—'with a rich interplay of oak and peat.'

'And on the palate,' adds Nick in measured time. 'Smoke and ash, sherried apple, leathery oak. Beyond sophisticated.'

'Exactly, and on the finish I'm getting the peat just edging past the brine.'

Amazing depth, we both agree. We sit back and savour.

'I wonder what Tennant has been up to lately,' says Nick, when the Scotch has done its deed and we're back to earth, left to transition our taste buds with pricey dark chocolate, a final celebratory indulgence.

Nick uses his phone to put an end to the guesswork. Surprise turns to exhilaration.

'Holy shit. He played Macbeth in London, with Cush Jumbo.'

'Cush Jumbo. No kidding. They must have been amazing together.'

'And get this. A performance was filmed. It's streaming in theatres starting in February.'

'We gotta go.'

'You're not kidding.'

February I never look forward to. Now there's a bright spot in the midst of all those hours of shovelling snow.

'And don't you love the name—Cush Jumbo.'

'Right up there with Carmel Ann Buttery,' Nick points out.

'And friends. Yesterday she sent me a complete list of the KNOT executive. You're not going to believe this.'

'Try me.'

'In addition to President *Carmel Ann Buttery*, born and raised in Gayside, we have . . . from the former Damnable—Vice-President *Roberta Freake*. From the once lovingly named Famish Gut—Secretary *Tryphena Loveless*. And lastly, and are you ready . . . ? Born in the former Scilly Cove and still resident there—Treasurer *Mortimer Auberon Coveyduck*.'

'Come off it, Dad. She's having you on.'

Bearing in mind that I've thought of *Sebastian Synard* as an embarrassing mouthful at times, I note, '*A rose by any other name . . .*'

'You got to admit there's an uncanny correlation between their quirky names and the quirky former names of where they came from.'

'Stranger things have happened,' I say.

'I'd say their own names are a weird incentive to believe everything was better in the past. A bizarre cult of some kind.'

I shake my head. He's been watching too much Netflix. 'This is Newfoundland. The closest we get to cults are those crazed bands of Costco shoppers. Except for those obsessive cooks who belong to the Cult of the Air Fryer.' I'm laughing.

Nick is only smiling. 'Something's weird. Trust me. Something's weird.'

'Time will tell. The dates of the conference have been confirmed. April 25th to 27th.'

'Where exactly in Dildo is it being held?'

'At the Come by the Bay Inn.'

'Enough said.'

TWO: DILDO

I'D BE THE first to admit there's much to be said in praise of Dildo. Or then again South Dildo, seven kilometres away. Or, for that matter, Spread Eagle, a further six kilometres along the shore. Together they add a certain sensuous undertone to the deep reaches of Trinity Bay.

The choice of Dildo and its environs as the location of the conference is clear affirmation of KNOT's core values—be damned the snide comments of outsiders, embrace the historic past, for the dogged residents will have the last laugh as the world comes to them in celebration of their fortitude.

And the choice of the Come by the Bay Inn as the opening session venue would seem an equally enlightened choice. My research notes that it has a total of seven ensuite rooms, all well appointed, together with an ocean-view dining room that, with the addition of extra chairs, can be quickly transformed into the meeting room for all of the conference participants, who I am informed will number between twenty and twenty-five.

KNOT has reserved the entire inn for the conference. Its rooms will accommodate the executive, the two guest speakers, and myself, and bring all the registrants together for Gutted: Fervent Focus on Newfoundland Toponymy.

An emphatic mouthful. Undoubtedly an attempt to give the conference academic credibility while at the same time luring the everyday amateur-history addict. We'll have to wait to see how well it succeeds, although Carmel Ann assures me that registrations, which have exceeded expectations, came excitingly close to the cut-off point.

So it's full speed ahead early this Saturday afternoon as I leave son and Gaffer, our warm-hearted mutt, contentedly ensconced at home in St. John's and set off for the Trans-Canada. It will take about an hour to reach the charming inn that will be my living and working quarters for three days, before hitting the road again for the anxiously anticipated "Grand Tour." In all I will be gone a week and, according to calculation, add roughly eleven-hundred kilometres to the odometer of the Mercedes-Benz Sprinter.

Yes, I was able to procure the beast. Not from your Avis or your Hertz or any of the run-of-the-mill vehicle renters. Rather, from a fine gentleman living in one of the more prestigious parts of town who listed his Sprinter on Turo, the online company that allows private individuals to rent their vehicles, kind of like an Airbnb for cars. Or in this case, a luxurious twelve-seater van.

Turo hit a high point post-COVID when the regular rental companies downsized, leaving few vehicles in their inventories. I recall checking the site at the time to see if it might improve my cash flow, given that the tour business had crashed and my Toyota was lying idle in the driveway much of the time. I abandoned the idea when I saw that potential renters had quite a number of newer, trouble-free models to choose from, including a Mercedes-Benz Sprinter.

It seems the owner has done very well by Turo, so well that the listing remained long after the masks came off and vaccination returned the vehicle-rental business to near normal.

The Sprinter comes with a hefty rental fee, but KNOT Treasurer Coveyduck didn't bat an eye. The exec must think it's worth every cent. Either they're used to affluence or, more likely, they're out to impress the government decision maker who will be joining them for the postconference tour.

Either way, I love it. Here I am, Ray-Bans on, cruising toward Dildo in the lap of luxury. Revelling in a ride that's incredibly smooth and spacious. Musically cocooned, experimenting with gadgetry that's landed me on an indescribable techno high.

Outside the Mercedes, it's April, the least uplifting month of the Newfoundland calendar year. Winter is in retreat, but it's not yet spring. In fact, April has been known to turn tail and dump a shitload of snow the day after you've unearthed the barbeque and lawn chairs.

But this year at least, so far so good. Fingers crossed, the remnants of our milder-than-average winter have pretty much melted and we're less than a week away from the more reassuring month of May. In fact, the farther I drive away from St. John's, the stronger the sun is blazing through the broad expanse of the windshield, bringing with it an even greater sense of optimism.

I turn off the Trans-Canada for the final few kilometres and into the parking lot of the inn, feeling like one of those chauffeurs about to drive up to some ritzy hotel to await the appearance of a famous starlet and her entourage.

In reality, however, it's Carmel Ann Buttery, rather older, with not quite the contours of your average starlet. And as for her entourage, they're a motley, discordant lot at first sight.

First impressions, as I have learned the hard way, don't always ring true.

The gentleman is the first to step forward and shake my hand. 'Mort Coveyduck. You must be Sebastian Synard.'

Our two names together suddenly seem relatively close on the quirkiness scale.

'Call me Carm if you like,' says Ms. Buttery. 'Mr. Synard, we finally meet face to face.'

Tryphena Loveless is next in line. She holds out her hand. 'I prefer Tryphena, but I can't escape Triffie, so I've given into it.'

Understandable. But either way, you'd think the parents could have worked at it a little harder when they named her, especially given the challenge of the surname. Nonetheless, Tryphena attempts a smile, although she's not exactly the life of a party it would seem.

And finally, 'You must be Roberta.'

'Bobbie, actually. Or Boo-Boo if you're so inclined.'

It bears repeating. 'Boo-Boo Freake, pleased to meet you.'

'I'm surprised you could keep a straight face.'

I chuckle, not quite sure what reaction she's expecting.

'Actually I was born Felicity Freake. I changed it.'

'I see.' Felicity is such a downer. Freake has its negatives, it's true, but it's a pretty common name in Newfoundland. I knew a Josh Freake in university. He was a popular guy. The girls were all over him.

'It's my stage name actually,' Boo-Boo informs me.

'Boo-Boo has made a name for herself in the horror-comedy movie genre,' Carmel Ann points out. 'Did you happen to see in her in *Death by Sirloin*?'

She's serious. I'd say the name alone opened a few doors.

'Can't say that I have,' I admit. 'Horror-comedy is not really my thing.'

'Eventually I'll move to LA, where actors, of course, are a dime a dozen. I made the decision to stand out from the crowd. I want to rebrand myself as Boo-Boo Freake from Damnable. Casting directors will eat it up.'

No doubt.

'Of course, I have a more altruistic motive. The original place name lays bare the struggle to settle in an inhospitable land. Instead of heedless optimism, it respects the raw reality of the past.'

Really? I'm left thinking there's more to Boo-Boo than is apparent on first meeting. Could that, in fact, be said of all four of the exec? What lingers behind their names might not be anything consequential, but then again . . . I'm nothing if not open-minded.

'How about we mark the start of our time together with an official portrait?' I suggest. A good first step, a reference point. 'How about a selfie in front of the Mercedes?'

They're all somewhat keen. The photo captures me and the KNOT foursome at this, the very beginning of our week together.

Left to right:

Carmel (Carm) Ann Buttery. A little less than average height, a good bit more than average weight—robust shall we say—undoubtedly with the instincts of a leader and the forthrightness needed for the role. Style sense off-putting: lemon-yellow faux-fur bomber jacket, black leather pants, and chunky, olive-green platform boots.

Tryphena (Triffie) Loveless. No longer smiling. The least comfortable, seemingly the most willing to fade from view, in her tightly belted tan trench coat and rimless eyewear. Mousy brown hair clipped back from her face with a few strands hanging loose. Both hands firmly in her pockets.

Mortimer (Mort) Coveyduck. The oldest and tallest by far. Has seen better days but is holding relatively strong. Likely slim in his youth, and still not much excess beneath his flannel shirt and down vest. A herringbone flat cap adds a certain aged jauntiness, as do the stonewashed jeans.

Roberta (*Bobbie/Boo-Boo) Freake*. Height on par with Carmel Ann, but, by a slim margin, she wins the attention-getting-dresser award. Enveloping her upper half is a vintage sealskin winter jacket, contrasting with mauve ski pants, skin-tight at the thighs, flared at the bottom and partially covering what appear to be camouflage combat boots. LA would be intrigued to say the least. Unfortunately, sealskin products are banned from importation into the US and LA is not known for its ski slopes. Still, good for a profile picture to enliven her resumé.

So there we stand, an unlikely lot knotted together.

Yet, I know better than to make assumptions, given my previous tour experiences. This much I've learned—common purpose makes strange bedfellows.

I recall a documentary about Bill Cunningham, the New York street-fashion photographer. He said it all. "Fashion is the armor to survive the reality of everyday life." I've survived without a great deal of fashion sense, but even I have had my moments. Maybe that's why I'm intrigued to discover what's behind the armour of the four who stood with me in front of the Mercedes.

Even more so because none of them makes much of a deal about the vehicle. Not yet anyway. Maybe they'll appreciate it more when we take to the open road. For now their focus is all about the conference. The opening session is scheduled for seven o'clock this evening.

At Carmel Ann's direction, I park the van in a more permanent spot, in line with her fiercely green Ford Fiesta and the black, nondescript SUV belonging to the inn's manager. I retrieve my overnight case and head inside, where I discover a bluster of activity. Everyone has a specific responsibility and is getting right to it.

'Your room and meals are covered,' Mort says, handing me a key. 'You're at the end of the hall and up the stairs.'

He's a little on edge. He's setting up the conference registration desk, not something he's used to doing it seems. There's a lot riding on Gutted: Fervent Focus on Newfoundland Toponymy. He wants it to go off like clockwork. Sorry to tell him, but KNOT's first conference is bound to be a learning experience.

As it will be for the other three. Having dispensed with their outer gear, Carmel Ann and Bobbie flutter about in free-flowing blouses, as colourfully as before, while Tryphena, in a black, vice-presidential pantsuit, stands in one spot consulting with the inn's manager. She introduces me to Jeanine, who has converted a portion of the dining room into conference meeting space, arranging chairs in proximity to a podium.

Two tables have been set side by side, presumably as a dining area for those staying at the inn, while the other three tables have been joined along a wall and covered with a lengthy tablecloth. A coffee maker sits alone at one end, in anticipation of the evening buffet.

I make my way down the hall, past five of the rooms and up the few stairs to where the final two rooms are located. The inn is nicely appointed, if you like French provincial, neutral colours, and damask wallpaper. Together with better choices of what I call Winners art. The inn aims for class if not a great deal of character. But, hey, I'm not complaining. The room is a significant step above my normal travel options. Though, I will admit, somewhat wasted on a single guy travelling alone.

I unpack my case, repositioning the clothes to the dresser drawers. I set out my newest acquisition—Glenmorangie A Tale of Spices—a significant step above my normal Scotch options. The retainer-funded bottle rests on an end table next to an armchair that's beside a window with a view of a sheltered arm of the North Atlantic. From this perspective, the inn is absolutely deserving of its four and a half stars.

I chose a Glenmorangie special release, not only for its reputation but equally for what I read on the box when I drew it from the shelf of the liquor store—"marrying four cask types for a mosaic of flavours." How weirdly appropriate, it struck me, for my days ahead ingrained with the four KNOT types, a mosaic of characters.

Will I find a book to pair with it for the whisky blog that has been an amusing pursuit of mine for several years? I mix Scotch with a good read for an online chit-chat I call *Distill My Reading Heart!* An endeavour that takes my mind off the less predictable aspects of my life, of which there never seem to be a shortage.

A "tale of spices" reappears downstairs. The KNOT team has assembled in a corner seating area for a mid-afternoon glass of wine. It's a respite after the flurry of preparation as well as sustenance for coping with the arrival of the conference attendees, all of whom are expected over the next few hours.

There's a vacant spot on one of the sofas, which I promptly fill. A bottle of Prosecco had just been uncorked, animating the conversation. I soon learn the team has also come together in anticipation of the arrival of the guest speakers, both due at any minute.

'Angelo Jones is one of the foremost authorities on toponyms,' notes Tryphena, who is seated next to me.

Pity he has such an unremarkable surname, I'm thinking. He might have trouble fitting in.

'He's written several books,' Tryphena says.

'Which you've read?'

'I prefer my books less academic.'

'You read a lot then?' I ask.

'As the mood suits me.'

I see. 'You have a favourite genre, Tryphena?'

'I'm into solo fiction.'

'I don't quite understand.'

'Solo fiction, novels generally, where the protagonist lives on her own. I mean, it doesn't have to be a woman, but obviously I'm steered in that direction.'

'I never knew there was such a thing,' I say.

'There are, in fact, subsets within the genre—historical solo, sci-fi solo, solo noir to name just a few. I'm not particular. I just need that sense of solitude.'

Sounds a bit confining to me.

'I like the comfort of an armchair—a book in one hand, a dram of Scotch in the other,' she says.

Well now. Isn't that a jolt to the grey matter.

'No kidding. What's your preference in Scotch?'

'Octomore has long been a favourite.'

Mine, too, except I can't afford it.

'Ardbeg Corryvreckan is a close second.'

Her disposable income is definitely a notch up from mine.

'I have to say I'm surprised,' I tell her. 'I'm a huge peat fan. Not many women I know go near it.'

'You obviously need to expand your list of acquaintances.'

If it had come from someone else, I might think of it as a come-on. In Tryphena's case, likely not. She has a stiffness about her that suggests intimacy is not in the cards.

She does, however, foster interesting conversation, more so than I would have expected. That first impression is now discarded. 'Any recommendations? Solo fiction I might enjoy with a Glenmorangie special release?'

She stands up. 'Let me get back to you.' She's off then, to some conference-related work in the kitchen.

It will be interesting to see what book she comes up with. Not that I'll likely read it. I have the sense that whatever Tryphena might choose would veer toward what used to be disparagingly termed *chick lit*.

That train of thought is suddenly displaced by the sight of a middle-aged man coming through the front entrance of the inn, rolling a piece of luggage at his side. He's either Angelo Jones, the toponymy scholar, or the government official, who I understand goes by the name of Richard Martin.

A second middle-aged man walks in the door just behind him, also guiding a suitcase. Once again it is either the academic or the bureaucrat.

Both are dressed in basic black. From all-weather hooded jackets and pants to boots to leather gloves. Arc'teryx vs Helly Hansen. Standing together, they look tentatively agreeable, presumably because they think of themselves as having the same solid fashion sense.

Both look profoundly unimaginative. If I were to bet, it would be Richard for the Canadian-founded Arc'teryx and Angelo for the HH.

For Carmel Ann, there are no questions of sameness. She's out of her seat, with a hand extending to the Arc'teryx. 'Richard, we're pleased to have you join us.' (A silent thumbs-up.) Richard's handshake is rather businesslike, less than the spirited response Carmel Ann might have been hoping for.

She smiles nevertheless. 'And thank you for waiting for Angelo,' to whom her hand quickly pivots. 'Sorry to hear the connection from Memphis was delayed, but I trust the limo from St. John's was comfortable.'

'I slept most of the way. I'm afraid I wasn't much company.'

'Not a problem,' says Richard.

Which leaves me with the impression that Richard likely preferred it that way. The two men, given their backgrounds, can't be as coordinated as their clothes suggest. I'd say there's a sizable toponymy gap between them.

Let's wait and see. Angelo is the keynote speaker for the opening of the conference tonight, while Richard is the after-dinner speaker for tomorrow night's closing banquet. At the moment all is convivial. Let's see if anything happens when the jackets and gloves come off.

Their arrival is a cue for the KNOT exec to get back in action. Mort deals with their registration, handing each of them a conference package.

Bobbie, standing by, holds two room keys in her hand. 'This way, please. My name is Roberta.' Perhaps having noted Richard's response to Carmel Ann, she keeps it businesslike. 'I'm your liaison for the conference. I'll direct you to your rooms.' They're off then, the revamped Boo-Boo leading the way. Her voice trails down the hall. 'If there is anything you need, you'll find my contact number in your package.'

For what it's worth, Ms. Freake, in my opinion, your best bet for place-name change is Richard. He's the one with the bureaucratic clout. If all you want is to see Damnable back in play, I suggest you make more of an effort to be congenial.

There I go—letting the other half of my working life influence my perspective. When I'm not tour guiding, I'm (believe it or not) a private detective. That's right, I make ends meet following the scent of fraud and deceit. You would be amazed at the lengths some people will resort to in order to get their way.

Forgive me, Roberta/Bobbie/Boo-Boo, I'm making assumptions. But to be honest, I don't really know you.

I'll start again from the beginning. I'll put aside your confusing network of names and settle on one. From here on in, you're Bobbie, and only Bobbie. As tempting as it is, I will not judge your character without verifiable evidence.

Bobbie returns, anxious to embrace whatever is next on her agenda. That would be the sound equipment, to confirm there won't be any last-minute glitches.

She displays an ease with audio hardware, as I have come to appreciate, having been commandeered to stand in various parts of the room so she can check the quality of the mics.

'Testing, testing, we're protesting, we're divesting, we're redressing.'

A step up from the mundane one, two, three . . .

She turns away from the mics to address me directly. 'When I first started acting, all I was getting were bit parts, so I'd look for a second job on sets as a sound tech. Anything to pay the rent. Then along came *Death by Sirloin*.'

And although she doesn't say it as such, the rest is history. It launched her career. It paid the rent and then some. 'Bobbie, is there likely to be a sequel?'

'*Death by Chorizo* goes into production next year. I play a down-and-out sausage-factory worker.'

It undoubtedly has potential in the horror-comedy genre.

'I'm perfecting a Spanish accent.'

'A bit of a challenge?'

'It's not meant to be entirely authentic. That's part of the humour.'

'Of course. And where does the horror come in?'

'Once again, meat tenderizers are not to be toyed with.'

I see a theme here.

'There's already talk of a third—*Death by* whatever. I haven't been told.'

Let me guess. *Death by Kebab*?

Bobbie, I'll say at this point, is a character. It's not a stretch to picture her embracing the eccentric backdrop of LA. What intrigues me is how someone growing up in relatively isolated, pocket-sized St. Chads could end up a hot property on the movie set of *Death by* whatever.

I suspect I'll learn more as the week wears on. As for now, I give her a resounding thumbs-up from every corner of the room. Once the conference starts, everyone might not agree with what's being said, but they'll certainly have no problem hearing it.

I return to the sofa, taking a few moments to relax and catch up on world events before the first of the participants arrive. A brief respite from the cluster of nonconformists surrounding me.

It turns out to be no respite whatsoever.

My phone screen reveals a bevy of lying, degenerate politicians, immoral multibillionaires, moronic conspiracy theorists. A world gone perilously mad.

Suddenly I'm starting to feel very thankful to be ensconced in rural Newfoundland. My companions might not be conventional, but neither are they fools drunk on power, out to release havoc on Planet Earth. I have every confidence that behind the outward appearance of each of the conference leaders is a decent human being.

And so, on with the show. I see that Mort could use a hand at the registration desk. I'll get to meet each of the participants and gain insight into just what type of individual willingly gives up a weekend in order to engage in the throes of toponymy.

Over the course of the next two hours, I come to the conclusion they fall into one of four whisky-cask categories:

The diehards. Who for various reasons are adamant that a name change was a grave error that needs to be corrected. They appear ready for a fight.

The curious. Who heard about the conference and are intrigued to find out what toponymy is all about. Yet to make up their minds where they stand. Mostly retired, with not a lot to do with their time.

The students. Who are majoring in geography at Memorial University and are here to learn about the issues around this aspect of what they term *cultural geography.* A field trip so to speak, with the benefit of good food and drink.

The reporter. Who amounts to the one media person so taken with the subject matter of the conference that she is eager to devote significant print and online space to it. She's a listener, here to weigh the arguments from all sides.

A diverse lot, which is a good thing. It looks like we're in for a lively exchange over the course of two days. Gutted: Fervent Focus on Newfoundland Toponymy might just live up to its billing.

All participants have checked in and received their conference packages. With outdoor gear removed and name tags affixed, they have time to refresh themselves and sample the array of food and drink options.

I'm impressed with the KNOT members' attention to detail. Rather than the standard *Hello: My name is* ___, the name tags read *How's it goin'? I'm* ___ *from* ___. Much more interesting. *Irma from Lushes Bight. Fred from Toogood Arm.* Even *Molly from Mount Pearl* has a certain charm.

And as for the array of finger foods and beverages, it's a patriotic assemblage sufficient to tempt every person in the room, whether local, expat, or perfect stranger. It's a Newfoundland scoff to define all scoffs.

Cod tongues topped with scrunchions, with a side of mustard pickles; toutens dripping with butter and molasses. Crab cakes, cod bites, dried caplin, smoked salmon, pickled herring, breaded shrimp, steamed mussels, grilled lobster luxuriating in lemon-garlic sauce. Bottled moose, bottled rabbit, bottled seal. Pork buns, molasses buns, raisin tea biscuits. Partridgeberry pudding, blueberry grunt, bakeapple tarts.

Good God. Is there no end to it? No, there isn't. Locally roasted coffee, locally foraged Labrador tea, Newfoundland cider, and iceberg water. And, of course, an array of craft beer from the Dildo Brewing Co.

Forty minutes later to a person the participants are satiated. The anticipation of the official opening of the conference is palatable.

The honour falls to Carmel Ann Buttery. The KNOT president stands at a podium before her seated audience.

'Thank you. Thank you. It is my absolute privilege to welcome each and every one of you to this, the first conference to bring together a group of civic-minded individuals in order to focus on the place names of our beloved Newfoundland with a view to ensuring they reflect their historic past. We stand firmly for tradition and not the transient whim of the trendy and superficial.'

A premediated, scripted mouthful. Mannerly but resolute, calculated to demonstrate that KNOT means business. Carmel Ann continues past her opening salvo, reading word for word to the end. Then, raising her head to scan the audience, she smiles broadly. Seemingly to reassure everyone present that, despite the serious intent, the conference will unfold in a spirit of goodwill and congeniality.

'We're in Newfoundland after all. We're never without our sense of humour.'

Relief all around. If anyone had concerns they had signed up for a morbidly earnest two days, they are becalmed. They smile back and take a reassuring sip of their chosen beverage.

'And now my friends, let me introduce our keynote speaker for Gutted, the extraordinary Dr. Angelo Jones.'

Ms. Buttery proceeds to do just that. It's a matter of formality, for we have all seen his profile on the conference website, and encountered it again in the registration handouts. Angelo Jones is a world authority on toponymy, whose most recent book—*What's in a Place Name? A Helluva Lot*—has been a huge hit with a broader public audience. No mean feat for an academic. A follow-up is due out next month—*So You Live in Cumming, Condom, or Dildo? So What?*

Which is a natural lead-in to his opening line. 'Good evening, everyone. Am I excited to be in Dildo, Newfoundland? You bet your Effingham I am.'

He's hooked us from the start.

'Yes, in fact, there's an Effingham in England, another in Canada, and a whopping four in the United States. So you might ask—just what's the effin' reason not one of them ever entertained the idea of changing its name? The answer is simple. They have history behind them. Place names don't appear without good reason. And neither should they disappear for no good reason!'

Angelo Jones has set his boundaries from the beginning. His talk is a compendium of stories—at the very least entertaining, often tantalizing, and on occasion rather odious—about potentially offensive place names from around the globe.

'Take Shitterton in England for example. A place name that dates back at least a thousand years. Derived from the brook that runs through the village, which in ancient times was used as a privy and was naturally called "the shitter." Is it any wonder the wooden sign to the village was stolen so often that the residents paid to have it replaced with an engraved slab of Purbeck rock? To quote the chair of the local council: "Let's put in a ton and a half of stone and see them try and take that away in the back of a Ford Fiesta."'

That yields a burst of laughter, crowned by Carmel Ann's high-pitched guffaw.

Then there's Brokenwind in Scotland, Bastardo in Italy, and Fjuckby in Sweden, which is a double whammy, so to speak, since *juck* in Swedish means *pelvic thrust.*

Our celebrated toponymist has broken wildly from the shell that seemed to encase him when he first entered the inn. Give the man legitimate cause to be provocative, and he'll spice things up with remarkable vigour.

The younger set in particular is loving it. Their constant chuckling encourages Dr. Jones to seek audience participation. An unsmiling international student from Germany takes to his feet and eagerly contributes *Titz und Weener* 'Of course the names are only amusing if you're English-speaking,' he said. 'As is the name of the street not far from where I live in Berlin—*Dickhardtstraße*. Only the tourists find it funny.'

'A very good point indeed. Which leads me to the basic premise underlying my toponymical research.' Jones pauses.

For effect, I assume. I wait, although not with bated breath.

'If the requirement for toponymical change is external pressure, perceived or implied, then it delegitimizes the requirement for change.'

There you have it in a jargonistic nutshell.

I'm seated at one end of the third and final row, and because the seating takes the form of a semicircle, I'm able to take regular glances at Jones's rival, Richard Martin, who is seated at the other end of the same row. He is not wearing a name tag, and next to him is the reporter, whom I noticed, when I was standing near her earlier, has opted for her own personal name tag. It reads *Heather Simpson, The Newfoundland Review.*

Neither of them has been sharing in the general congeniality. The reporter, I assume, for professional reasons. The bureaucrat, undoubtedly because he's not impressed. In fact, his facial expression veers toward a scowl at times. It could be plain smugness. It could be that he finds the sexual innuendo unnecessarily repetitive. Or lacking scholarship. Whatever the reason, he's not enjoying himself.

Angelo Jones was handpicked to reinforce KNOT's perspective, and he's done just that. He has little more to offer, and ten minutes later, he ends his presentation to enthusiastic and sustained applause.

Carmel Ann joins him at the podium to offer thanks and present him with a gift—a first-edition copy of *Place Names of the Avalon Peninsula of the Island of Newfoundland*. 'By the legendary Newfoundland toponymist E.R. Seary, dating from 1971 and in pristine condition.' She's thrilled.

The man of the hour is equally thrilled. He sets the book reverently aside and throws the session open for questions from the audience.

The reporter is quickest off the mark. 'What would you say to people who contend that the name of their community brings unwanted attention, to the point it disrupts the very peace that drew them to settle there in the first place?' She has not been drawn in by the adoration running through the audience. She's maintained her journalistic neutrality.

In her lap is a small device that I assume has been in recording mode since the session began. It awaits his response.

Jones readjusts his posture, having been caught off guard by the studious tone of her question. 'I would say do as Dildo did. Embrace the moment. Go all in. Build it and they will come.'

A titter runs through the audience.

At which point Richard Martin slips quietly, and largely unnoticed, out of the room.

The reporter ignores the lewd undertone of the response in favour of follow-up questions. 'But what if that is not the route they want to take? What if they want less attention, not more?'

'Then I say blandness scores big time. Mediocrity comes out on top.'

She stops at that. Unsatisfied I assume. If I read her body language correctly, she has been far from impressed by Angelo Jones. I assume that, as a reporter, she will retain an open mind on the subject matter at hand, at least until the conference has ended, yet the fact that she chose to sit next to the man's rival could be taken as leaning toward the partisan. I'll be very interested to see what exactly shows up in *The Newfoundland Review.*

The questions that follow are less contentious. Jones relaxes and as the Q & A comes to an end, he's basking in even more animated applause. When it dissipates, Carmel Ann leads him to a table stacked with copies of his book, and the eager lot wishing to purchase autographed copies.

Except for those of us staying at the inn, the conference attendees eventually drift away, either to nearby accommodations or back to their home communities. They'll reassemble for the ten o'clock session in the morning.

I make a point of speaking to Heather Simpson as she dons her winter jacket and woollen beret. 'I'll see you in the morning?'

'Yes. Thank you.' She adds, 'You're a member of KNOT, I take it?'

'Not really.' I explain my role in the conference and what will follow it.

'I just assumed . . . Interesting. And you're spending all that time with these people.'

There's something in my smile that likely tells Heather more than I intended.

'You're in for a thought-provoking few days.'

Interesting choice of words. I shrug.

'Do you mind if I ask you something . . . off the record?'

I have no idea where this is going, but I have enough self-control not to put myself at odds with the organization that hired me. 'Sure.'

'Did you know that the major funder of KNOT has a vested interest in one of the proposed place-name changes?'

It's come out of nowhere, and I don't quite know how to respond. 'Do you mean that the person stands to gain financially if the name is changed back to what it was?'

'You're familiar with Lonz Littlejohn?'

'The movie magnate. Of course.' Who hasn't heard of Lonz Littlejohn? Born and raised in Newfoundland, made it very big on the big screen, including an Academy Award nomination for *Time Off*, the sequel to *Calling in Sick*. Critics say he's redefining the comedy genre.

'And you know where exactly he was born, where he lived until he was fifteen when his family moved away, where he's said his sense of humour had its foundation?'

'Somewhere in Trinity Bay, I thought.'

'Winterton,' she says.

'You mean . . . '

'The former Scilly Cove.'

'Lonz Littlejohn from Winterton.'

'Lonz Littlejohn from Scilly Cove sounds so much more fitting,' she says. 'Especially since he's named his production company Cinema Scilly Cove. From what I gather, he's got his mind set on reversing the place-name change. Money talks. And he's got plenty of it.'

'Do you mind telling me how you know all this?'

'KNOT obviously doesn't lack for money. A conference like this doesn't come cheap. You'd be surprised what keynote speakers charge these days. KNOT doesn't have a lot of members, and the ones they do have didn't appear to me to be particularly well off.

'That was the starting point. The rest was research. Mortimer Coveyduck was forthcoming when I pressed him. You remember Uncle Mort in *Time Off*. He was based on Littlejohn's real Uncle Mort.'

Heather's tenacity has reaped rewards. But there's more.

'And Aunt Bobbie, Uncle Mort's ex-wife.'

'You're kidding. Bobbie Freake is Lonz Littlejohn's aunt?'

'On his mother's side. Remember the classic lines from the movie—when the guy says "Bob's your uncle." And the other guy says, "It's not that simple, you twit. Bobbie's your aunt."'

How could I forget?

We leave it at that. For now. 'See you in the morning.' We agree to meet for coffee before the conference resumes.

Well, that was a rewarding few minutes. Heather Simpson is an intriguing woman.

It's too early to retire to my room for the night. I nab one of the few beer left on the food-and-drinks table and head for the seating area. With the last of the conference participants having now dispersed, the exec wander over, eager to debrief.

Carmel Ann takes the lead. 'Angelo will be along shortly. I contacted Richard but he's decided to call it a night.'

In other words, he has no intention of spending more time listening to Dr. Jones run off at the mouth.

Carmel Ann continues, 'To judge by the audience reaction, the keynote went very well.'

'Absolutely,' says Bobbie. 'Angelo nailed it.'

'I was inspired.' That would be Tryphena. Which I find odd. I don't recall seeing her in the audience. Unless she heard him from the open door of the kitchen.

As for Mort, 'I sent Lonz a text. Told him it was worth the investment. Only a matter of time before it turns a profit. You know, language he understands.'

Carmel Ann raises her eyebrows, I assume to ward off Mort venturing into KNOT topics not meant for my ears. I play dumb.

In fact, I go one better. 'The man's a raconteur, which he's managed to balance with his academic attributes.'

'Very nicely put, Sebastian.'

BS actually.

It seems Mort has trouble keeping a lid on the fact that Lonz Littlejohn is paying the shot. Not that it should be concerning to me. If it's his money that's upping my bank account, so be it. It can't be much more than a drop in the bucket to what he made from *Time Off.*

Speaking of making a good wage, here comes Angelo Jones—in fine form, having reduced the stack of books considerably, and ready for yet more adulation to come his way.

'How good of you to join us,' says Carmel Ann, moving

slightly to one side, with the hope that he'll sit next to her. He does, which means he's next to me as well.

I extend my hand to him. 'I don't think we've formally met.'

We exchange names. He's waiting for more. A compliment on his keynote, I assume.

'I'm arranging our excursion following the conference.'

No response. 'Sebastian operates a tour business,' Carmel Ann notes, to fill the gap.

'Very good,' he says. And stops at that, turning to the others.

If I wasn't impressed before, I'm even less so now.

Says Tryphena, 'Dr. Jones, are you pleased with how you were received?'

Just what he needs. 'Very pleased. Although there was bound to be a least one naysayer in the audience. She has her role to play. That's par for the course.'

I hate to tell him, but Ms. Simpson was doing more than playing a role. She was doing her job.

That being said (although not out loud), I have to admit (to myself at least) that I'm in a bind. On the one hand, I'm finding the person seated next to me a blowhard, while on the other, I agree with his position. Place names should retain their historical context. To replace them with something insipid and characterless betrays the lives lived by our ancestors.

'I was delighted by the response of the students,' says Jones. 'I appreciate broad-mindedness.'

That you do when it's accompanied by loud applause.

I'm not sure I can take much more. I lean forward on the sofa. 'Well, folks, I think I'm off to get some shut-eye.'

'Sebastian,' says Bobbie, 'it's still early. Don't be a turd in the punch bowl.'

A what? Did I hear that right?

They're all chuckling. Mort, in fact, snorts. 'Leave it to Boo-Boo,' he manages between his guffaws.

'Stay right where you are, Sebastian,' says the woman in question.

She nods to Tryphena, who goes off and is back in short order with a tall, black bottle, which she plants on the coffee table. 'Who besides Sebastian is up for a dram of Octomore?'

To add to the plot twist, the keynote speaker rises to the occasion. 'I'm a bourbon man myself. Hold that pose.' He's gone and back in no time with (I can't believe it) a bottle of Pappy Van Winkle, hands-down the most prestigious bourbon I've ever laid eyes on. 'Everyone call me Angelo, by the way.'

'Wait. Wait,' declares Mort. He rushes off, only to return with a swank, decanter-shaped bottle of El Dorado 25 Year Old rum. 'Compliments of Lonz.'

Now then.

The evening has lost its reserve. KNOT is letting down its hair. And with incredible flair.

No more calling it a night. There's three remarkable reasons to stay put and accept the offer of a glass from the tray that Carmel Ann has fetched from the food-and-drinks table.

Normally I avoid mixing my drinks, but no way am I about to pass up such a stellar array. When the spirits move, follow. Savouring every sip along the way.

And—lo and behold—over the course of an hour, Dr. Angelo Jones is much easier to ignore.

His egotistic self hasn't toned down any. But when the focus is what's landing on my taste buds, I'm good at turning the rest into background noise.

The time to call it quits does eventually come.

It's nearing midnight. I set sail for my room.

As I make my way up the stairs, my elbow catches the arm of someone going down. 'Oh, sorry.'

'Are you sure you're okay?'

'I wasn't looking where I was going. Searching my pockets

for my room key. My apologies . . . Mr. Martin.' He must be the occupant of the room next to mine.

'Not a problem.' Unsmiling. Intensely sober.

Not sure what he's up to this time of the night. No one has seen him since he walked out of the keynote earlier in the evening. He's fully dressed, so he obviously hasn't really called it a night.

'I'd rather you call me Richard.'

'Sorry again, Richard.'

'Good night.'

'You wouldn't happen to be interested in a nightcap? I have a bottle of pretty good Scotch.' Some compensation for running into him.

To my surprise, he responds, if somewhat hesitantly, 'Thank you, I would.'

We reach the top of the stairs. I open the door and Richard follows me inside. 'Have a seat.' I motion to the armchair by the window, then reposition a second chair across from it.

I always travel with two Glencairn glasses. I never know when I might be sharing what with whom.

'Just a taste,' he says. Which suits me fine, considering what I've already consumed.

In any case, I get the feeling that Richard accepted my invitation for a reason other than the whisky.

He takes a sip. It goes down without comment. But not without a question. 'Do you really feel this conference makes any sense?'

It's a loaded question that I hesitate to answer. My own sip doesn't go down so easily.

'I understand that you have been hired by the organizing committee,' he adds. 'Can I assume you're not a member of KNOT?'

That question I'm willing to answer. 'Yes.'

'But you have an opinion about its agenda?'

I fail to see where he's going with this. Is he feeling isolated? Is he looking for an ally? He seems somewhat unnerved.

'An opinion? Yes, you could say that.'

Richard takes another sip. 'I won't ask you what it is.'

Okay, so is there any point in keeping it from him? My alcohol-loosened tongue says no.

I've said it before, and I might as well say it again, 'Take Baytona. I cringe every time I hear it.'

'That's your response. The residents of the community have a different perspective.'

'As does KNOT.'

'But they're not the people living there.'

'Except for Carmel Ann,' I note, 'who just went back and once again calls it home.'

'In which case Ms. Buttery can do her best to convince her fellow residents to revert back to Gayside. Good luck with that.'

True enough. I might cringe, I might think it was a godawful choice, but it was done as a result of a democratic vote.

'So does the government have any control whatever? If some cliffside community gets it in its head to change its name to . . . I don't know . . . Palm Beach. Could the government refuse to accept it?'

'Aside from the obvious reason, it bears no relation to local history or geography, so yes, it would be refused.'

'But what if the original name did just that? Scilly Cove, for example, was named after the Isles of Scilly, off the southwest coast of England and known to the earliest settlers. So why was it allowed to be changed?'

'It was more than a century ago. I doubt there was much in the way of regulations. Why was it changed? I assume because the *c* is silent and they got tired of outsiders making fun of it.'

'Silliness if you ask me.'

'Nevertheless . . . they felt they had the right to change it.'

'To Winterton. After a disgraced prime minister of Newfoundland—James Spearman Winter. They could at least have had some imagination and changed it to Spearman Sound. That would have had a bit of life.'

Richard fails to see the humour.

The man's got several days ahead of him, cheek by jowl with KNOT. He'll be miserable the whole time if he doesn't loosen up.

'So, this is how I see it.' (The topper of Glenmorangie is having its way with me.) 'The members of KNOT are well meaning. They're out to change minds. From their perspective, that's a plus for culture, heritage, tourism, whatever. You might think they're extremist. I don't. Let them see how far they get. If, in the end, they're able to persuade the residents of a community to revisit the name change, more power to them. If not, they'll just have to swallow their pride, and KNOT will die a quiet death.'

'So what is this conference? A way of getting public attention?'

'Exactly.'

'One reporter is not going to do it.'

'It's a start.'

Richard's not convinced. But at least he shrugs. Which is a step up from blatant cynicism.

'I'm meeting Heather Simpson in the morning for coffee before the conference resumes. I'll put it to her. Let's see what she thinks. She likely knows the public mood better than we do. Let's see if she thinks KNOT has any future, or if it's just a flash in the pan.'

He takes it for what it's worth, then stands up to leave.

That's it. He's gone and I take over the armchair, left to thinking there's not much more to do but go to bed. Except finish what's in the glass and sit for a few minutes, wondering why I got mixed up with this peculiar cast of characters.

Why? Because it pays the bills and then some, including the purchase of what just went so smoothly down my gullet.

THREE: SCILLY COVE

DAY TWO OF Gutted. A change of scenery. Dildo makes way for Winterton.

Winterton, further along the Trinity Bay shore, also has a long and impressive history, in this case going all the way back to the 1600s. And an equally impressive modern one, what with the recent initiative of Greg Wells (multi-award-winning music producer, member of the Order of Canada, and all around good-hearted guy) to purchase a local church building and turn it into a non-profit music venue and recording studio to raise money for the town. Very unlike Lonz Littlejohn's apparently self-enriching antics.

I did question the wisdom of the KNOT executive in separating days one and two of the conference by fifty-seven kilometres. Splitting the venues, they reasoned, between Dildo (which had kept its name) and Winterton (which hadn't), would reinforce the impartial nature of the conference. Let's wait and see how it pans out.

The dining room at the Come by the Bay Inn has been reset to its original purpose, with seating for six to enjoy breakfast in front of the bank of windows that look out on the waters of Dildo Arm. The seventh, Tryphena, had breakfast earlier and has gone ahead to

Winterton to get started on the catering arrangements for the day.

The sunlight glints off the water, highlighting a couple of boats as they head out to the fishing grounds. Spring, the season of new beginnings, is in the air. Seated at opposite ends of the table, Angelo and Richard appear willing to put aside differences for the sake of KNOT and the array of traditional Newfoundland breakfast items spread before us.

Wisely, Carmel Ann uses the food to nudge the conversation away from anything likely to engender disagreement.

She sweeps her hand in the direction of a platter heaped high with toutens, that all-time favourite breakfast—or any time of the day, actually—treat. 'Sebastian, would you be so kind as to relate to Angelo the history behind the touten?'

Ah, the history behind the touten. Now *there's* an innocuous topic if there ever was one. I'm more than happy to bolster the congenial tone Carmel Ann has set.

'Ah, the touten—cut from fresh dough that is mixed the evening before to rise near the wood stove overnight. Traditionally fried in rendered pork fat and served with melting butter and a healthy drizzle of molasses. Angelo, let me say that this particular local gastronomic delight is not to be confused with the damper dog, or the doughboy, or the flummy, or—of course—the infamous bangbelly.'

This generates a weak smile from Angelo. The others laugh out loud.

'If indeed you do find yourself confused, then I suggest you consult the *Dictionary of Newfoundland English*, where you may find yourself further confused since there is no right way to spell the word—*touten* with an *e*, or an *i*, or *o*, or *a*. Practically any vowel will do. And its derivation? Unknown.'

As a toponymist and an author, Angelo prides himself on being a wordsmith. As an academic, he prides himself on never being confused.

He has a comeback, one that I should have anticipated but didn't. 'Is there any place name, past or present, that uses the word *touten*?'

Richard, coffee cup to his lips, rolls his eyes.

'Not that I am aware of,' I answer quickly, hoping it goes no further.

I should be so lucky.

'How about it, Richard?' Angelo calls down the length of the table. 'Does Touten Cove ring a bell? Or Touten Arm? Or Touten Tickle?'

Four of us like to think Angelo's words are no more than a skewed attempt at humour. We chuckle good-naturedly.

Richard does not. 'We avoided naming our communities after food,' he answers drolly. 'Generally it's not very appetizing.'

We chuckle even louder.

'But you did name one after lack of it,' Angelo proclaims. 'Famish Gut!'

Richard is turning red. With exasperation, I assume.

'That's right,' responds Bobbie, before Richard has the chance. 'And there is a Plum Point,' she adds hesitantly. 'But then again, I'm not sure if it qualifies.'

'Let's have a go at the toutens then,' Carmel Ann says, eager to quell the discord. She forks one onto her plate and encourages the others to follow suit. She pours on the molasses and passes the jar along.

Let's stand back for a moment. What am I witnessing here? Indignation caused by a humble wad of fried bread dough? How fractious are we that the lowly touten can spark a rise in tempers? Get real, folks. Life is too short to get on like this over such trivia.

Let's finish breakfast, don our outdoor gear and head out into the sunshine, take a deep breath, and board the Mercedes for the trek to Winterton. Put differences aside, sit back, and take in the beautiful world around us for the next hour as we head north along the shoreline of Trinity Bay. I'm more than happy to provide insightful commentary to keep your minds on our shared love of this splendid seascape rather than anything that serves to split us apart.

'We're now entering the quiet, peaceful community of Whiteway, where both fishing and lumbering have been a mainstay since the 1850s. This time of the year, the lobster season is at its peak, and if you look out your windows to the left, you'll see a fisherman heading out to haul his pots.'

'That's Shag Rock sticking up there in the middle of the harbour,' declares Angelo.

He's very quick with his smartphone. Nevertheless, I maintain my instructor voice. 'Indeed so. Jutting high and fiercely out of the water, a stunning landmark to say the least.'

'I'm surprised there wasn't a petition to change its name,' the shit disturber says. '*Shag* has several meanings, but one, of course, is sexual intercourse.'

Will someone do us all a favour and put a gag on the man?

'You mean as in *shag* off, you *shagger*?'

That from Richard, precise and emphatic. A blatant outburst to bait his rival.

'Then of course,' counters Angelo, 'there's *sheep-shagger*.'

'You're not implying . . .'

'Okay, folks, back on track.' I barge in before things go off the rails entirely. '*Shag* in Newfoundland refers to a seabird. It's the local name for the double-crested cormorant.'

'Exactly,' Richard declares. 'It's got nothing whatsoever to do with sex. We have at least a half-dozen geographic features termed *shag*, including Shag Island, Shag Ledge, and Shag Islands Shoal.'

There you have it, Angelo. Case closed.

Not quite. 'Whiteway was originally named Witless Bay,' he counters. 'Residents renamed it Whiteway, after a former premier. Renamed because they didn't have a *shaggin'* sense of humour.'

'Renamed,' Richard fires back. 'Because there was another Witless Bay in another part of Newfoundland. Their mail was always getting *shagged up*.'

Dear God, is there no end to these petty outbursts?

'And now,' declares Carmel Ann, in a voice to drown them all, 'we're about to pass through the delightful community of Cavendish. Wow! Look to our left, folks. A bright purple house with a stunning collection of yard art!'

Good deke there, Carmel Ann.

'I love the purple,' declares Bobbie.

And wow, it's all quite amazing actually. I slow down so everyone can get a good look.

Newfoundland outports have their pockets of homemade yard art, but this collection is the wildest I've ever laid eyes on. I especially like the tiers of car tires painted red, purple, yellow, and turquoise. And filled with Tonka trucks, overhung with metal baskets stuffed with stuffed toys. And the UFOs on the roof of the house. Outrageous. I love it.

'Quite silly, if you ask me,' says Angelo.

Nobody's asking you, numbnuts.

'We had a Scilly Cove,' says Richard. 'Its name was changed.'

'Cavendish,' I inject, to override them both, 'was renamed in honour of Sir Cavendish Boyle, governor of Newfoundland and author of the "Ode to Newfoundland," our official anthem.'

At which point Carmel Ann starts to belt it out. Eventually, everyone except Angelo joins in:

'When sunrays crown thy pine-clad hills
And Summer spreads her hand
When silvern voices tune thy rills
We love thee smiling land,
We love thee, we love thee,
We love thee smiling land!'

It's a brilliant tactic. No Newfoundlander can be anything but roused to patriotic euphoria. Disharmony fades, leaving Angelo mute and in awe of the fervour that has spread to every corner (except his) of the van.

That heartfelt fervour continues as we drive to the next three communities along the shore—Heart's Delight, Heart's Desire, and Heart's Content. Yes, indeed, somewhat of a love nest of Newfoundland toponyms!

I beam with pride every time I pass this way—such unabashedly bright, joyful, uncontentious place names! Each has its separate history, of course. In one case, a history that set the eyes of the world upon it. And ours on something unquestionably positive for a change.

'Here in Heart's Content, in 1866, arrived the SS *Great Eastern*, at that time the largest ship ever built. It had laid an undersea cable across the Atlantic, the end of which was hand-carried ashore, the very first telegraph connection between Europe and North America, an incredible milestone in the history of technology!'

I take a quick side trip from the highway and park in view of the handsome red brick building, the cable station that had served the world, now a museum. 'As I like to say, Angelo, for decades, the *heart* of global telecommunications.'

The man can't be anything but impressed. I return to the highway with faith there will be no further toponymic taunts.

Playing it safe, I pass Turks Cove on mute just in case

it should remind someone there was also a place named Turks Gut, whose residents changed its name to the rather colourless Marysvale. (No offence intended, I'm sure, to the Barbary pirates who ravaged the coast of Newfoundland in the seventeenth century, and for whom it had been named.)

In any case, Winterton is only a few kilometres away. With directions from Mort, I drive past the government wharf with its colourful cluster of longliners, and on past the town's acclaimed Wooden Boat Museum, before arriving at the conference venue for day two, a spiffy new community centre—Stagehead Scilly Cove.

So much for KNOT's argument about impartiality.

'Officially it's a bit of a mouthful,' says Mort. 'We calls it *The Hall*.'

Mort is building a reputation for putting his foot in his mouth. Carmel Ann frowns in his direction. They rented the venue, without doubt, to support KNOT's effort to reinstate the town's original name.

'A terrific step forward,' says Carmel Ann, as we cast eyes on its full name in gold letters above the front entrance. 'So much more captivating than Winterton Community Hall.' (Or, which goes without saying, The Hall.)

'Lonz came up with the name. And since he paid the whole shot for its construction, nobody said boo.' Mort laughs out loud. 'That was the joke around town.' He laughs again.

A stupefying, eye-opening tidbit.

For my benefit only it seems. Carmel Ann is already out the door, anxious to get the conference program in motion. The others weren't far behind, met by several participants who have already arrived, including the troupe of enthusiastic geography students and their instructor.

The students immediately gravitate to Angelo, drawing him to one side, their phones ready to record his responses to their questions, no doubt for inclusion in upcoming class presentations.

The rest of us make our way inside. Stagehead Scilly Cove is what you could call a dinner-theatre space. It seems every town in Newfoundland of any historic significance has a dinner theatre to draw in tourists over the summer months. Nothing too tragic. Laughter the key ingredient. Generally, it combines performance and music into a lively show that interprets local history and goes down well with the traditional Newfoundland meal laid out before them.

I gather from Mort that Lonz not only designed the theatre space but is also its artistic director. He spends most of the year in Florida working on films but still finds time to mount a Stagehead production that runs through July and August.

'He was determined to do something different,' Mort eagerly explains. 'No way was it going to be like every other dinner theatre in the province. The man's a renegade. No two ways about it.'

From what I gather, Lonz Littlejohn combines theatre and film. Exactly how, I don't quite understand, given Mort's disjointed explanation. He's off then to make sure the tables and chairs have been arranged in the configuration KNOT specified.

I, too, have a job. I've been seconded by Bobbie again to help her test the sound equipment. She's gaga over the range and quality of the set up. 'Leave it to Lonz. He's spared no expense.'

I'm increasingly intrigued by this Lonz Littlejohn. Though he's thousands of miles away at the moment, his presence is unmistakable. He's the topic of conversation when I've finished up with Bobbie and have connected with Heather Simpson. We've poured ourselves coffees and found a spot for a private chat.

'I've been to the dinner theatre,' she says. 'I've written about it for the *Review*. Quite impressive, actually. Live theatre combined with live video projection. In one sequence, the actors are in a kitchen making Jiggs Dinner—peeling carrots, turnips, and potatoes; slicing the cabbage; preparing the pease pudding and figgy duff. They're singing and dancing as they do it, while on the screen above them is projected video of the dinner being consumed by the audience as they watch the performance on stage.'

I can't quite imagine it myself. But looking around me, I feel I'm being steeped in the aura of Lonz Littlejohn. Winterton/Scilly Cove is undoubtedly under his spell.

As confirmed by the fact that a dozen or more people have arrived unexpectedly and are now standing in line at the registration table. Mort, it seems, knows them all.

'Locals,' says Heather. 'I remember from the conference publicity there was the option of signing up for day two only, at a special reduced rate for residents of Winterton.'

Mort is excited to see the sudden influx. As are Carmel Ann and Bobbie, who are busily putting out extra tables and chairs.

'These are decision makers,' Heather points out. 'If Winterton has a referendum to become Scilly Cove again, then these are some of the people who will vote.'

'And who will influence how their neighbours vote.'

'Precisely. Grassroots democracy in action.'

I'm also excited. I had expected a tedious day of KNOT preaching to the converted, but it's turning into an open demonstration of just how much traction its ideas actually have. 'If, at the end of the day,' I say, 'these residents are not convinced they want to return to the era of their ancestors and embrace the founding name, then KNOT might as well pack it in and head home, tail between its legs.'

Heather nods in agreement. She, I can only assume, is also excited. Being the impartial journalist that it appears she is, she's not inclined to articulate her enthusiasm. There is, however, a gleam in her eye. The media thrives on controversy. I sense she's thinking this could result in a significant boost to the readership of *The Newfoundland Review*.

We take to a table and wait for the action to unfold. I notice Richard Martin has withdrawn a chair from one of the back row of tables and placed it at a distance behind the bulk of the audience. He sits alone, notebook in his lap, pen poised to record what might impact his after-dinner speech this evening.

'Richard seems to have calmed down,' I say. 'He's looking more relaxed.'

'He'll like the fact that all these local residents have turned up,' Heather says. 'He thinks he has support for keeping the name as it is.'

'I wouldn't be so sure. Lonz Littlejohn holds a lot of clout in this town. Standing here, we're surrounded by tangible evidence of that. There's a lot more money where this came from.'

'But he's thousands of kilometres away. His voice is a distant echo at the moment.'

Not quite.

The moment everyone is seated, the screen above the stage comes alive. Backed by a dramatic orchestral soundtrack, a sweeping drone panorama of radiant Winterton in midsummer descends to end squarely in front of Stagehead Scilly Cove.

The doors to the venue open, and the image on the screen transitions to a live-action shot from the back of the theatre, weaving in among the tables, quickly capturing each person in the audience (notably Carmel Ann waving wildly and Bobbie blowing kisses).

On screen (shot in Florida to judge by the palm trees in the background) is Lonz Littlejohn. Waving wildly back at Carmel Ann. Is he taped or is he in fact live? Who can tell?

There's no question, however, where his solidarity lies.

His red T-shirt proclaims *Make Us Scilly Cove Again!*

His red ball cap emphatically declares *MUSCA!*

The music is almost drowned out by cheers. Lonz Littlejohn raises two clenched fists. A sizable portion of the audience reciprocates.

He slowly transitions into a serious charmer. 'Dear friends and neighbours. Although I am not with you in the flesh, I am with you in spirit. In the spirit of love for the community that touches our hearts, that touches our minds. As you sit in Stagehead Scilly Cove in Newfoundland and I in Cinema Scilly Cove in Florida, I sense a current connecting us, the current of commitment to a crusade.'

Heather and I turn to each other, eyebrows high and rigid.

'A crusade to return to the glory of the past. A crusade to bring us to a true referendum, undefiled by fraud. A crusade to Make Us Scilly Cove Again!'

'Dear God,' I whisper, 'the man is an egomaniac.'

'He's playing it like he's the *chosen one*.'

'Remember, dear friends and neighbours, when the time comes to vote, you are also voting for the construction of the Arena Scilly Cove. The plans for which are already on the drawing board.'

Arena Scilly Cove? Is he serious? A town this size can't support an arena. But with Littlejohn, I guess it's ask and you will receive.

'An NHL-sized ice surface for half the year, a state-of-the-art film studio for the other half.'

Give me a break.

'It's nothing less than out-and-out bribery,' says Heather as she writes furiously on her notepad. No more furiously than Richard Martin is writing in his.

'Unbelievable,' I mutter. 'You can't make this shit up.'

'He can and he did. And people are swallowing it whole.'

She's right, to judge by the raised fists pumping the air.

The promises continue to spew from Lonz's mouth. 'Scilly Cove will become another Dildo, only more fantastic. Believe me, tourist traffic will be incredible. It will be such a beautiful thing. There'll be so much winning, you'll be saying, "Please, Lonz, please. It's too much! I can't take any more winning. There'll be winning like no one has ever seen winning before."'

Knowing my Newfoundland history as I do, I recognize repetitive, self-indulgent rhetoric. From a chocolate factory to greenhouses for growing cucumbers . . . Projects undertaken to win votes, only to fizzle into bankruptcy.

I wish I could pull the plug on the man. Instead, I grit my teeth and hold out to the final, repetitive declaration.

'Make Us Scilly Cove Again!' And, for good measure, Lonz shouts it a second time, even louder.

The live-action camera pans the audience, zooming in on several raised fists before fading to black.

'Thank God that's over.'

Unfortunately, it's not. A tone has been set. The conference sessions turn into little more than endorsements of KNOT's perspective.

Carmel Ann Buttery's forty-minute session—"Virgin Arm, Come By Chance, Blow Me Down . . . Who's Next?"—starts out civil enough but soon turns into a diatribe against anyone willing to entertain the faintest notion there could be a legitimate reason for changing one of the names.

Likewise, "Take My Place Name in Vain," led by Bobbie Freake. Which is initially somewhat level-headed but takes a turn for the worse when the geography instructor stands up to make the point that 'the place names assigned at birth, so to speak, might not correspond to how the residents feel about their community as it matures. Is it fair then not to allow toponymical transmortification?'

Whoa. But if her aim is to incite heated argument, countering what she sees as bias taking hold of the conference, her approach fails miserably.

'What's she goin' on about?' someone mutters.

'Is that even English?' grumbles another. Just loud enough to be heard.

The instructor raises her voice. 'Just because you don't understand—'

'Now folks, there's no need,' Bobbie says. 'Free speech is embedded in our constitution.'

But the damage has been done. Two factions have emerged—one with an impassioned support of KNOT, and one not so sure what they support. As the conference sessions unfold, one after another, interest in Richard Martin's closing address and the Q & A to follow has steadily built. Martin's the power broker, the government official who sets the course for toponymy in the province. Whether all he's seen and heard will have any influence on his decision-making is unknown. His speech could prove a turning point. Or it might not, leaving KNOT stymied in its quest for change.

When the final session ends, I respond with a huge, if inaudible, sigh of relief. I've wallowed in toponymy but have managed to emerge with my common sense intact. I felt the cultish lure but didn't drink the Kool-Aid.

I have a whisky sour instead. It's cocktail hour, a very welcome respite, an hour to relax and unwind from the afternoon's excesses before dinner and Richard's much-anticipated address.

KNOT, in one of its more inspired decisions, hired a mixologist for the occasion, a specialist in cocktails using only alcohol and bitters made in the province, including the very first distilled, barrel-aged whisky. We've been producing vodka, gin and rum for years, plus aquavit and liqueurs.

Heather has trouble making up her mind. How about a Salty Seaman made with Seaweed Gin, or a Harvest Moon made with Gunpowder & Rose Rum? She finally decides, taking a sip as, together, we move aside to make room for the overeager students next in queue. Heather comes away with an espresso martini made with Evening Tide Vodka and Bonavista Coffee Liqueur.

'An exceptional mouthful,' she declares. 'I'm beginning to think the food and drink at the conference have surpassed the intellectual content.'

'KNOT hasn't done itself any favours by being so aggressive.'

'It's bound to backfire.'

We'll see. We'll see how Richard responds. I notice he's not around. I suspect he's passed up cocktail hour in favour of returning to his room to fine-tune his remarks.

In the meantime, the caterers—the same folks recruited for the dinner theatre in the summer—have preparations for the meal well in hand. Under Mort's vigilant eye, the tables have been rearranged at the front of the hall. They are covered with tablecloths printed in an abstract teal pattern of ocean waves and topped with centrepieces artfully fashioned with driftwood, shells, and beach pebbles.

And, according to Heather, 'Flowering succulents.'

Flowering succulents. Who knew? To my way of thinking, all too crafty.

Obviously, this is going to be a step beyond the outport cold-plate supper I had envisioned. Great. I for one wasn't particularly looking forward to bright pink beet-and-potato salad.

Soon cutlery, matching cloth napkins, and an array of glassware are arranged to make up six place settings at each table. Following a chart she holds in her hand, Bobbie places a handwritten place-name card at each one.

I can only imagine the flurry of activity in the kitchen, with Tryphena, whom I haven't seen all day, in the thick of it.

The dinner guests have taken to the back of the hall, cocktails in hand, chatting up a storm as they are meant to do, in anticipation of the call to be seated for what KNOT has billed a "Right Proper Scoff."

Heather scans the crowd, looking for the instructor who, this morning, had been the object of ridicule. I did notice that, over the course of the day, she wasn't the least intimidated, never hesitating to pose still more questions.

We find her sipping a colourful concoction through a straw inserted among various bits of semi-submerged fruit.

Heather introduces herself. 'I'm with *The Newfoundland Review*. Do you mind if I ask you a few questions?'

'Not at all.' The instructor extends her hand. 'Jasmine.'

'Would you mind telling me how you became interested in cultural geography? And would you mind if I record this?'

'Not at all.'

Heather takes out her recording device.

Jasmine takes another sip. I can see in her eyes that she has a story to tell. 'I emigrated to Canada with my parents when I was eight. I was born in the Philippines in a place called *Sexmodán*.' She spells it. 'Of course as a child, I didn't think the name was peculiar. But years later, when I was a teenager, the family went back to visit and I discovered the spelling had changed. To *Sasmuan*.' She spells it as well.

'I see. Changed because of the sexual connotation?'

'Well, sexual connotation for English-speaking tourists. To begin with, the former name was Spanish, a colonial corruption of the original Indigenous word for *meeting point*. So when it was changed in 1991, at least it was changed back to its pre-colonial origins.'

'I see,' says Heather. She's pleased with Jasmine's response, devoid as it is of the overcharged emotion that dominated much of the day.

'In each case,' Jasmine says, 'there are at least two sides to the issue, often more. If there's a proposal for change, or for reversal of change, then, as I tell my students, there needs to be open and rational debate by the stakeholders.'

I'm equally impressed. Once past the jargon, there's a lot to be said for academia.

'Winterton is a prime example. I'm personally not keen on the name, but the local residents are the stakeholders. If they're happy with it, then what reason is there for them to change it back to what it was?'

I can't resist. 'Unless someone manages to persuade them they're *not* happy with it.'

'There is that.'

His name goes unspoken.

Not for long.

The door to the hall is thrown open, and Lonz Littlejohn himself bursts into the room!

Eight hours ago, a visual image of him had faded to black, and now here it is reanimated, in the flesh in real time! Tanned and wearing a MUSCA ballcap. Arms extended as if wanting to embrace us all.

Jasmine, though just as startled as we are, has words for it. 'Opportunity knocks. Grab it or you lose it.'

'In other words,' I speculate, 'the guy boards his private jet in Florida and four hours later arrives in St. John's. And in Winterton an hour after that.'

'Or less,' notes Heather, who, as have I, just spotted the Newfoundland Helicopters logo on the jacket of a fellow who walked in the door behind him.

There's an intense hullaballoo building around Lonz Littlejohn's sudden arrival. It's almost as if he has appeared by magic, by special effects of the sort endemic in the movie industry.

The helicopter pilot hands him a leather duffle bag. Littlejohn unzips it and removes a stockpile (or should that be an arsenal?) of red ball caps, identical to the one covering his head.

He takes a cap and hurls it into the air above the crowd. On its descent, a fellow snatches it and crowns himself. A solid segment of the crowd goes wild.

For his supporters, it's a feeding frenzy. For the rest of us, it's a bombastic display unbefitting the occasion. When several caps fall at our feet unclaimed, Lonz Littlejohn finally gets the message that not all the people in the room share his enthusiasm.

That only adds fuel to his message. 'We come together, my friends, to share one heart, to share one home. We fight, fight, fight! Together we'll Make Us Scilly Cove Again!'

I doubt this one-sided, theatrical display is what KNOT had in mind. It certainly drives a stake into any pretense of a balanced atmosphere leading up to Richard's after-dinner speech. The last thing the exec must want is for him to get his back up.

Carmel Ann is making an attempt to calm the waters. She directs one of the catering staff to gather the excess caps and return them to their owner, while encouraging the crowd to find their places at the tables. She approaches Lonz with a firm smile.

Having roused his base of supporters, Lonz suddenly adopts a subdued demeanour, smug in the belief that the evening will unfold in his favour.

An additional table has been set out behind the others to accommodate Lonz and Sven, his pilot, together with a third person who has just swept in through the door.

'Ahhh, Charmaine,' he intones. 'Meet Carmel Ann.'

"Ahhh" is right. Charmaine is tall and encased in a red, full-length Canada Goose parka. The fur trimming the hood covers all but her face, heavily tanned and shaped by overly thick lips, taut cheekbones, and meticulous makeup. Botox has had its way with her.

The parka extends to matching red, high-heeled leather boots. She unzips the parka with flair, slips out of it, and hands it over to Carmel Ann, who has offered to hang it in the cloakroom, eager as she is for all three to be seated and no longer the centre of attention.

But that's not about to happen. The red leather extends up Charmaine's legs and over her knees, ending just short of a tight, spaghetti-strapped, sequined, black mini dress. An eyeful that lures repeated stares as she and her companions are directed to their seats. There's no shortage of individuals eager to take the bait.

Challenging as it is, I'm not one of them. My assigned table is in front of the stage, well away from the one put in place for Lonz and his companions, together with, I now notice, one Angelo Jones. Which is more than a little interesting.

I'm sharing the table with Heather, seated next to me, and surprisingly, with three of the KNOT exec and the man of the hour, Richard. I can only assume that the combination was intended to give him the opportunity to relax, enjoy his meal, and not feel additional stress leading up to his speech. Thus, the exclusion of Angelo and the substitution with Heather, although where Angelo ended up may not have been his choice. Or was it?

Mort takes charge of pouring the Vinland White that stands in waiting in the centre of the table. It's a Newfoundland-made dandelion wine. He half fills each glass, sits back down, and raises his own. 'Cheers, everyone!'

I take a tentative sip. Our climate is not conducive to grape growing, so we make do. That dandelions are locally termed "piss-a-beds" only complicates identifying the wine's flavour profile. 'Intriguing.' To say the least.

'Well, folks,' continues Mort, 'we're definitely in for a treat. I had a peek in the kitchen, and they're dishing up something very special.'

Carmel Ann smiles in Richard's direction. 'In keeping with a very special day and a very special guest.'

Richard is not easily won over by flattery this late in the game. But he does return her smile, though it's noticeably restrained.

'The cooks have pulled out all the stops,' says Bobbie, renewing the enthusiasm.

The servers make their appearance in smartly coordinated outfits, although they leave me thinking—why red? Yet another endorsement of MUSCA?

Heather, leaning my way, is thinking the same. 'At least they avoided the logo.'

Fortunately, the more intense focus is what they hold in their hands. As the head table, so to speak, we are the first to be served.

And special it is. An appetizer of cod chowder made, according to the server, 'the traditional way, with Purity Hard Bread and Mount Scio savoury.' Authentic. And, on my first spoonful, delicious.

Followed by a beautifully arranged seafood platter—lobster, crab, shrimp, oysters, scallops, mussels—with crusty bread and pickled vegetables, and a range of dipping sauces. Brilliant. We're speechless.

All except Richard. 'I have an allergy to shellfish,' he informs us, "us" being myself and Heather. The others appear to be aware of it already.

Thus the stuffed chicken breast, green beans, and scoops of pink beet-potato and yellow pineapple-corn salads on the plate in front of him. I can't say I'm envious.

The seafood platter has taken hold. Although—like the others at the table, I assume—I am embarrassed to be feasting on such riches while the guest of honour gets to work his way into stuffed chicken. Even if it is topped with a creamy mushroom sauce "made with real wine," as the server had pointed out.

'I've learned to live with it,' Richard assures me. 'Enjoy your meal.'

I do my best. I have to admit that, once I turn my full attention to what's before me, I'm thoroughly appreciating every mouthful. Our ocean temperatures might not be conducive to swimming, but by God, they make for some of the best seafood on the planet.

And as for the dessert that follows—chocolate mousse sprinkled with partridgeberries and Newfoundland sea salt . . . What can I say except 'To die for.' Everyone agrees.

Again, all except Richard. He's not allergic to chicken but looks as though he's just not feeling up to it. He's looking rather unsettled—in anticipation of the reception he fears he might get for his upcoming speech, I assume.

Carmel Ann notices it too. As soon as the servers begin taking orders for coffee and tea, she gets to her feet. She invites Richard to do the same, rather than allow him time to become even more anxious.

'Shall we?' She extends an open hand toward the podium. They head to the stage. With Richard ahead of her, Carmel Ann looks back at her colleagues and takes a deep breath. Rather unnecessary to my mind. Whatever he has to say, Richard's sure to be diplomatic.

As he stands to the side of the podium, with Carmel Ann about to introduce him, he's not looking the least combative. In fact, if anything, he's distracted and inattentive.

'Good evening, everyone. As president of KNOT, let me say how pleased we all are to welcome Richard Martin, representing the provincial government department responsible for the administration of the Geographical Names Act.'

At this point, one would expect Richard to be looking his professional best. Instead he's holding a handkerchief to his mouth and coughing. Rather loudly.

Suddenly, without warning, the folder in his other hand drops to the floor. He presses the empty hand against his chest.

Carmel Ann quickly turns to him. 'Are you okay?'

He lowers the handkerchief. His lips are swollen. The effort it takes to catch his breath makes answering impossible.

Abruptly, he slumps to the floor.

'Oh my God!' exclaims Carmel Ann. 'He's fainted.'

I push back from the table and head to him. Fainted?

I think it could be something more. I sink to my knees and draw his hand away from his face.

'Anaphylaxis!' I yell into the crowd. 'Someone call 911!'

I bend closer to him. 'Richard, your EpiPen, where is it?'

He's already feeling for the pocket of his suit jacket. I push my hand in ahead of his and retrieve a small red case bearing a white cross. I quickly unzipper it and withdraw the thick tube. I know exactly what to do.

I encircle it with my fist, pull away the blue safety cap, and jab the orange end straight through his trouser leg and into his thigh.

In the commotion, I miss hearing the click that indicates the skin has been penetrated and the epinephrine injected. After five seconds, I pull the pen away. Its orange tip extends to cover the needle. I relax my hand.

I'm staring incredulously at the tube. It's marked *TRAINER*.

I didn't hear a click because there was no needle! It's not a real EpiPen. It's a facsimile used for training purposes.

'Richard, listen to me! Do you have another EpiPen? A real one.'

He can't answer. He's vomiting.

A search of his other pockets produces nothing.

'Check his outdoor coat,' Carmel Ann yells to Mort. 'It's hanging in the cloakroom. Anyone know if he had a briefcase? Check that too.'

Which all takes valuable time. And in the end produces nothing.

Richard looks very much worse. His tongue and throat are swollen. He struggles to get his breath. I check his pulse. It's far too high. His face is flushed, telling me his blood pressure has likely spiked.

Winterton has its own ambulance service. Where the hell is it?

'The ambulance is on its way to the Carbonear hospital,' yells a woman in the audience, one of the dozen local residents on their phones. 'Someone in Heart's Content had a heart attack.'

Jesus.

'The next closest place with ambulance service is Old Perlican,' the woman says. 'They're just about to leave. If we're lucky, twenty minutes to get here.'

Richard could be dead by then.

In the meantime, another woman knows someone in Winterton who she thinks carries an EpiPen. She's on the phone to her.

The woman at the end of her call is shopping in the Walmart in Carbonear.

Jesus.

But the shopper knows of a kid in New Chelsea who has a severe allergy to nuts.

'Yes, yes! Call the parents!'

New Chelsea is ten minutes away. Add five minutes to that by the time Dougie, the kid's father, is on the road in his pickup with a double dose, hazard lights flashing. 'Dougie's a friggin' fast driver,' yells someone else.

Not as fast as the person driving the ambulance, which is coming from the same direction and which 'just passed Dougie outside Hant's Harbour.'

The play-by-play drives up the tension. Richard is barely conscious.

The ambulance tears into Winterton and into the Stagehead parking lot. Thirty minutes have elapsed since the call to 911.

Two emergency responders race through the open door. A now-unconscious Richard Martin finally gets the jab.

The click resounds through the hushed silence. The click that could save his life. Followed by a tentative sigh of relief.

A quick check of Richard's vitals. 'Priority One! Let's go!' Within seconds he's on the stretcher, wheeled out the door and into the ambulance.

I stand in the parking lot, in the midst of all four of the KNOT executive, watching as the ambulance tears away, lights flashing, siren blaring.

'At least twenty minutes to get to the Carbonear hospital' is the consensus from the mass of onlookers behind us.

There's no chance to catch our collective breaths. The ambulance is barely out of sight when into the parking lot (light and siren inactive, thankfully) comes an RCMP patrol car.

From it emerge two officers. 'We understand from 911 there's been an incident. We were just in contact with the ambulance. We assume everything's under control.'

Carmel Ann steps toward them. 'Yes, Officer. It appears the gentleman in question, Richard Martin, suffered an allergic reaction. The ambulance responded accordingly, and the necessary medication was administered.'

Only after that abbreviated version of what actually happened does she introduce herself. Constables Blanchett and O'Rourke do the same.

O'Rourke returns to the vehicle to take a call while

Carmel Ann fills Blanchett in on what exactly has brought everyone to the hall.

She just finishes up when Constable O'Rourke returns.

O'Rourke is looking particularly serious. 'Bad news, I'm afraid.'

A brief, considerate pause.

'Cardiac arrest. The gentleman in question could not be revived.'

Richard Martin is dead.

FOUR: BIDE ARM

IT'S A SHOCKED and troubled collection of onlookers that makes its way inside, following a sympathetic yet firm directive from Constable Blanchett.

'Please return to the seats you occupied when the incident took place,' he announces. Then, following a brief word from Carmel Ann, adds, 'Working staff, please assemble outside the kitchen.'

At that point, Constable O'Rourke, last seen returning to the police car, presumably to contact her superiors, enters the hall. She and Blanchett find space for a private discussion. I make my way to what had been the head table, now—like all the others—bearing only a tablecloth whose seas suddenly look turbulent, with a sad-looking centrepiece caught in its throes.

From the constables' huddle comes a further announcement. 'As you are fully aware, an incident took place that has resulted in a death. No doubt there will be an autopsy to confirm the cause. The RCMP will initiate an investigation to eliminate the possibility of foul play. Until we do, we are treating this as a potential crime scene.'

A wave of disbelief sweeps across the room. Overreaction on the part of two inexperienced cops? Or are they dutifully following orders from higher-ups?

'Dear God, you can't be serious.' A voice from the crowd, pitched high above the others.

Blanchett is quick to react, his tone intensified. 'You were all witnesses to the incident. You are to remain where you are until the head of the detachment arrives. He will decide how we proceed.' My questions answered.

'How long will that take? My wife has kids to put to bed.'

Blanchett might tolerate the appeal, but he dismisses it as trivial. One thing he does know—domestic obligations can't dictate the timeline of police investigation.

'Staff Sergeant Larkin is on his way. I suggest you all relax.'

That's not about to happen, even though the group at each table draws in on itself, having come to the conclusion it's not in its best interest to challenge the officer any further.

I'm suddenly struck by the fact there's not a MUSCA cap to be seen, including the one that appeared to have been permanently implanted on the head of Lonz Littlejohn. Dodging undue attention no doubt. Nobody, especially Littlejohn, wants the RCMP to question whether they might have been at odds with Richard Martin. They're safe for the moment, while the constables hold the fort until the top brass arrives.

In the meantime, the constables are looking efficient under pressure, recording details about what took place in order to brief the staff sergeant when he does get here.

Carmel Ann is their informant of choice, given she is the chief organizer of the conference and was on stage with the deceased when he collapsed. I refrain from inserting myself when she points to me in the course of answering their questions. The police prefer it when you wait your turn. I'll be the focus of their attention soon enough.

As it happens, they don't get to me before the main door to the hall swings open and in walks the man we've all been waiting for. The constables are at his side before he's made to feel uncomfortable by the eyes that have turned en masse in his direction.

The trio get up close and private, a preliminary exchange, as expected.

But before long, they decamp so the staff sergeant can address the anxious audience. Standing alone, he cuts a striking figure. Of course the uniform helps. As do the couple of inches above six feet. And the handsome face that means business. He could be a poster boy for RCMP recruitment.

'Do you recognize him?' Heather whispers to me.

'No. Should I?'

'He played the arresting officer in *Time Off*. Lonz flew him down to the movie set for that one scene. He had maybe two lines, but with long close-ups as he stared down the guy who played Uncle Mort.'

There's no time to linger on the side story, intriguing though it is.

'Thank you, everyone, for your patience. I'm Staff Sergeant Larkin and I'm head of the RCMP detachment in Harbour Grace, whose responsibilities include Winterton. Constables O'Rourke and Blanchett have briefed me on what has taken place up to this point. I'll explain how we proceed from here.'

An arm rises in the audience, belonging to the same guy with the wife whose kids have yet to make it to bed. 'Yes?'

'How long do you expect this will take? Some of us have commitments.' Noticeably less combative.

'As you must realize, you are witnesses in a potential crime scene. As such, we need time to access which individuals among you had direct contact with the deceased. If you did not, then you will be free to go shortly, provided we have your contact information should we need to be in touch with you at some future date. Understood?'

Indeed so. No more raised hands.

'Good.'

In the course of looking about the room, Larkin's eyes fall on Lonz Littlejohn. A slight double take at seeing the man who apparently gave him a moment, brief though it was, of fame.

Lonz raises his hand ever so slightly, only a forefinger above his head. 'If I may. I just want to say how impressed we have been by the professional manner in which the investigation has been conducted so far. I am sure I speak for everyone when I say the RCMP have our full cooperation.'

A mellowed Littlejohn, devoid of the histrionics we witnessed earlier. Rather smarmy in my opinion. Anything to remind the staff sergeant of who was responsible for his face hitting the big screen.

Larkin doesn't know quite how to react. He can't be seen as being anything but even-handed. The yet unexplained fate of the dead man takes precedence. In the end, he merely nods and moves on.

'I understand that, except for the kitchen staff, catering staff, and Ms. Buttery, everyone in the room is now seated exactly as they were when Mr. Martin collapsed. If you are not, please identify yourself.'

Again a scan of the room. Again no raised hands.

'Very good. Except for those seated at the head table, is there anyone who interacted with Mr. Martin from the time the conference sessions ended to the time he took his seat for supper? I understand there was what is referred to as a *cocktail hour*.'

All hands immobile. Which is not something I would dispute. I have no recollection of Richard mixing with anybody during that time. I can't even recall seeing him in the room.

'I seen him outdoors.' It's one of the catering staff. 'I was stood up outside the side door havin' a smoke when he came out and went off down the road. Looked to me like he was goin' for a walk.'

Duly recorded. 'Did you speak to him?'

'No, sir.'

'Did you see him return?'

'No, sir. I was only out for a few draws. I was back in again in a couple of minutes.'

I would say it was Richard's opportunity for some fresh air to clear his head before giving his speech. Plus an escape from having to engage in small talk with people he didn't know or who were on the other side of the toponymic fence. In any case, he was back and taking his seat at the head table, and at that point at least, seemingly clear-headed and ready to take to the podium when the time came.

After more private words with the constables, Larkin looks ready to deliver a pronouncement. 'I have access to the contact information each of you gave when you registered for the conference. If that has changed, or if for any reason you failed to register, you are to see one of the constables immediately. As for everyone else who is seated, except for those individuals either at the head table or staying at the inn in Dildo, you are free to go. Thank you again for your patience.'

'If I may, Staff Sergeant.' It's Carmel Ann, making her way quickly to where Larkin is standing. 'I would like to have a brief word with the participants before they depart.'

'Certainly.'

She looks out on the group. 'This has been a very upsetting conclusion to our time together.' She takes a moment to compose herself. 'When I approached Richard to attend the conference and to give the closing remarks, he readily accepted, even though he knew his perspective on Newfoundland toponymy would likely not be that of many of the participants. He was steadfast in what he believed and would have done an excellent job of articulating that viewpoint if he'd had the opportunity.'

Her voice weakens. 'We are very sorry he did not.' She stops to regain her composure. 'We are very sorry to have lost such a gentleman under these dreadful circumstances. If you would, please stand for a moment of silence in the memory of Richard Martin.'

The rustling as we stand eventually gives way to stark silence. I can't help but admit there is some chance, remote as it may be, that not everybody will be sorry about what happened. No doubt the three police officers are weighing the same possibility, depending on the results of the autopsy. But even at this point, there are a number of unanswered questions about how Richard Martin came to the end that he did. And like it or not, until they're resolved, we are standing in silence in a potential crime scene.

'Thank you.'

And with these words from the president of KNOT, the vast majority of the conference attendees disperse.

Some more quickly than others. I notice the father with the kids yet to make it to bed is deep in conversation until the wife practically drags him out the door. And, no surprise, Lonz Littlejohn is shaking the hand of the staff sergeant. A bit too vigorously to be anything but another reminder of just what a unique and mutually beneficial relationship they have. Charmaine is in on the act as well.

'They haven't met before,' Heather tells me. 'She's new.'

New and all smiles. Either there's something about a man in uniform, or it's to Charmaine's advantage to act like there is. I go with the latter.

The conversation becomes inappropriately animated. The couple will depart Stagehead Scilly Cove on very good terms with the Royal Canadian Mounted Police.

'You know where you can reach us,' Lonz says to Larkin as they head out the door, behind the pilot carrying the tightly zippered duffle bag.

'Of course.'

In the lull that follows, Heather whispers, 'You've noticed the house on the point, overlooking the ocean? With the red metal roof and all the windows, and the turret that resembles a lighthouse.'

I haven't, as yet. 'That's his?'

'His summer retreat. He refers to it as "the Shed."'

'His attempt at humour, I take it.'

'One hopes.'

Larkin interrupts. 'I would ask that all those remaining, except for the kitchen and catering staff, take a chair and seat yourselves in the back of the hall. I'll be with you shortly.'

We dutifully follow the instructions while the officers huddle with the others outside the kitchen.

The kitchen itself has to be the major focus of the investigation, presumably if there were leftover portions of what made up Richard's meal. As for what remained on his plate, it likely ended up in a garbage bin with the scrapings from all the other plates, cross-contaminated sludge.

The kitchen will be for a forensic team to deal with, if one is warranted. As of now, it's locked and the key put in the open hand of the staff sergeant.

Larkin's questions for the kitchen and catering staff generate a steady stream of note taking by the constables. No doubt Larkin goes straight to the crux of the matter. Where did the ingredients for Richard's meal originate? Who prepared it? Who else had contact with it? What route did it take from the kitchen to the head table? What was Richard Martin served for dessert? What did he have to drink?

Eventually, Larkin terminates the fact-finding session. Constable O'Rourke hands around a clipboard and pen, presumably for their contact info. In due course, the kitchen and catering staff will find themselves at the detachment in Harbour Grace to answer more questions and provide written statements.

Except for Tryphena, they are free to leave. They don their coats and slip out into the night—upset and relieved in equal measure.

Larkin turns his attention to us. To judge by the no-nonsense tone of voice he expects a greater grasp of police procedure. 'It's getting late. There are still matters to be addressed. Let's maintain our focus and deal with them as efficiently as possible. Agreed?'

No small talk. No digression. 'Agreed.'

He checks the notes Blanchett has handed him. 'Ms. Buttery, why, given your guest speaker's allergy, was the choice made to serve shellfish for the meal?'

It's something she had to be expecting. 'Actually, it was a point of debate among the executive. We seriously considered pan-fried cod, but then we were serving cod chowder as an appetizer. There were two of us in favour of stuffed chicken breast for everyone and two of us who argued strongly that, if we're to maintain our theme of Newfoundland food then shellfish would be the logical choice, given the abundance of it in the local area. In the end the shellfish won out, once I had contacted Mr. Martin and he assured us his allergy was not airborne and he was agreeable to being served an alternative meal. Isn't that right, Triffie?'

The spotlight turns to Tryphena, who had spent the whole day in the kitchen, as the one responsible for coordinating the meal preparation.

Tryphena is slow to answer. She's feeling the added attention. 'We were extremely careful to isolate the preparation of Mr. Martin's meal. In fact, the separate portions were prepared well beforehand, covered and refrigerated. Just prior to serving, the chicken breast and sauce were reheated and arranged on a plate together with the cold salads.'

Not sounding particularly appetizing, but as I recall, Richard consumed much of what was placed in front of him.

Larkin is not about to get into the particulars of the meal preparation. That's for another time, involving the whole of the kitchen staff.

I'm next on the agenda.

'Sebastian Synard?'

'Yes.'

'I understand you are the person who administered an EpiPen just shortly after Richard Martin collapsed. Or what you thought was an EpiPen.'

'That's correct.'

'Weren't you aware it was a so-called "trainer"?'

'In the commotion that followed his collapse, my only concern was to activate the EpiPen. I grabbed it without taking time to examine it closely. I was only aware it was a trainer after the fact.'

'I assume you were familiar with the procedure for administering an EpiPen,' says Larkin.

'Yes, I am certified for standard first aid.'

'And what happened when it was discovered that the EpiPen in question was ineffective?'

I lay out the details, up to the time the ambulance arrived.

'And how much time had passed from the point at which Mr. Martin collapsed?'

'Roughly thirty minutes.'

It's as if I sounded a death knell. Larkin says nothing.

Everyone in the room knows what he's thinking. The same as what we've all been thinking. Richard Martin's chances of survival lessened with the passing of each of those thirty minutes.

Larkin abruptly moves on. 'Angelo Jones?'

'Yes, sir.'

'You were not seated at the head table, I understand, even though you were a guest speaker at the conference.'

'Yes, sir.' Stiffly compliant.

'Do you mind telling me why?'

'I was invited by Mr. Littlejohn to sit with him,' says Angelo.

'You are friends?'

'Not as such.' The man hesitates. He glances at Carmel Ann.

'If I may . . . Mr. Littlejohn generously provided the funding to bring Mr. Jones from his home in the US to the conference,' Carmel Ann tells him. 'He sponsored him, you could say.'

'I see. And that funding covered the speaker's fee as well?' Larkin turns from Carmel Ann back to Angelo for the answer.

'That's my understanding, sir.'

Not the precise answer Larkin wanted. He looks again to Carmel Ann.

'Yes.'

I'm hoping the next question is how much. There's a pause, but in the end, no such luck.

Larkin continues. 'The meal, then, was an opportunity for you and Mr. Littlejohn to get to know each other.'

'Yes, sir.' A note of relief, with just a shade of enthusiasm for the suggestion. It seems that Angelo doesn't want to sound anything but preoccupied—as we all are with the tragedy at hand.

'And that left an additional place at the head table, which was then occupied by . . . '

Larkin checks his notes. 'Heather Simpson.'

Heather raises her hand, just enough to be noticed.

'I understand that you're not a member of the organizing committee,' Larkin says. 'Would you explain your role at the conference?'

'I'm a journalist, here at the invitation of the conference organizers. My intention is to write an article for *The Newfoundland Review*.'

'I'm not familiar with it. A local magazine?'

'Yes. Long established. In fact, in two years we celebrate our centenary.'

Her answer would suggest that the officer is not by birth a Newfoundlander, or if he is, not a literary one. Either way, he and Heather are not off to a good start.

'And you still plan to write your article, despite what has happened?'

'Yes.'

'I suggest, Ms. Simpson, that you exercise discretion, bearing in mind we're in the midst of a police investigation. I caution you to stick to the known facts and avoid speculation.'

She's not pleased. Suddenly she has her reputation to defend, and that of the magazine.

'*The Newfoundland Review* prides itself on accuracy. No way am I about to deal in speculation and conspiracy theories.'

That ups the ante abruptly.

The staff sergeant doesn't quite know how to respond. I'm thinking he hasn't dealt with many journalists, especially any that fall within the outspoken female category. It's as if his reputation as the quintessential Mountie has been challenged.

When in doubt, ignore and press ahead, as if nothing of importance has been said.

Larkin checks his watch, then returns his attention to the group. 'This concludes my questions for this evening. I understand from Ms. Buttery that you will be returning to the inn in Dildo. You are to remain there until I arrange to meet with you individually, at which time I will require a witness statement outlining your role during the conference and any contact you might have had with Richard Martin. Is that understood?'

It is.

'I have a point needing clarification.' It's Heather, clear and distinct.

'Yes.'

'I do not have accommodation at the inn in Dildo. My intention is to drive to my home in St. John's.'

Larkin takes a moment. 'On condition that tomorrow, you drive back to the detachment in Harbour Grace, at which point I'll expect a witness statement and will likely have further questions.' The Mountie is back in the saddle.

'Very well,' she says. 'I'll likely have a few of my own.' He shouldn't expect a smooth ride.

Nevertheless, that's it for now. Pack it in, lock the door, and, temporarily at least, go our own ways.

I manage a few private words with Heather. 'Let's keep in touch. I'll be interested to know where your questions lead.'

'Likewise.'

Likewise?

A knowing, ready smile. 'You do have another life,' she says. 'More than one of the cases left a trail on the internet.'

I shouldn't be lost for words. I shouldn't be surprised at her journalistic instincts working overtime.

'Your secret is safe with me,' she adds.

'Thanks.' I work at looking cool about it all.

There's a moment for us to absorb the realignment of our relationship.

How would I put it?

The *investigative* journalist makes a deal with the tour guide/undercover *investigator*. For their mutual benefit.

Depending on where the questions lead.

It's a solemn trip in the dark back to Dildo. No hearts contented, delighted, or for that matter, desired. No Shag Rocks visible. Cavendish yard art brightly lit, but its entertainment value lost on us.

The seat formerly occupied by Richard Martin radiates a ghastly silence that no one dares to break. We press on soundlessly, made all the more conspicuous by the fact that Mercedes-Benz engineers have managed to suppress almost every last decibel of exterior noise.

It's with great relief that I finally turn into the parking lot of the Come by the Bay Inn. The passengers methodically exit the van. And, once inside the inn, but a few words are exchanged before everyone makes their way to their respective rooms, closing the doors quietly behind them.

As I head down the hallway, the last to retreat for the night, I imagine the strains of some musical composition to break the sombre silence. It would have to be a requiem for a conference.

Once inside, I give Nick a call. Let's just say he's now in possession of a basic, abbreviated version of what has happened since I left home. He's desperate with questions, which I convince him are best left for another time. It's sleep I need. Plus I have a witness statement to write.

If there's a brighter note to bring closure to the day, it's to be found in the bottle sitting on the end table next to the armchair. A stout pour of Glenmorangie now in the hand of a showered, towel-wrapped tour guide/undercover investigator.

My dual identity is in sudden need of prioritizing. The tour-guide component is literally on the rocks. For all intents and purposes, the Grand Tour is dead in the water. Not only has it lost a key member of the entourage, but Staff Sergeant Larkin decreed that the remaining six stay within quick contact, at least until he has the results of the autopsy.

On the other hand, the investigator component is advancing rapidly. Even without the autopsy report, I detect the scent of foul play. What's with the trainer EpiPen? Why, despite all the precautions, did the stuffed chicken breast, sauce, and/or salads cause not only an allergic reaction, but a severe allergic reaction? And above all, why would anyone go so far as to cause the death of conservative toponymist Richard Martin?

And *why*, sure as hell, leads to *who*.

Who? Someone known to the victim. Someone at the scene of the crime. Someone with a motive. In other words, basic Private Investigation 101.

Tomorrow will be pivotal. Depending on what the KNOT exec decides to do in lieu of the Grand Tour, it may be the only time the remaining six of us are together. And in that case, a singular opportunity for me to flick a few switches to see if anyone lets drop something that might lead to the reason for Richard's demise.

Am I jumping the gun? Better that than hanging back half-cocked.

A second shot of Glenmorangie.

It's going to take dexterity on my part to work so many angles without raising suspicion. Especially with five personalities in play. I'll miss having a fresh set of eyes and auxiliary brainpower.

That would be my prior partner in crime, Mae. Let's just say the last case left the two of us at investigative odds, complicated by the fact that Mae is also my significant other. We managed to keep that relationship intact, although the flare-up took its toll.

I'm not sure Mae's prepared to restart the role of PI teammate. Or if I'm prepared to risk another feud, this time with the potential of putting our relationship permanently on the skids.

Another shot of Glenmorangie.

On the other hand, it could just be the peace offering needed to reinvigorate the romance, the passion, the love affair gone somewhat tepid.

That's being optimistic, but hey, if the stir beneath the towel says anything, it's that life is too short to play safe.

Hit me with your best shot. Fire away.

I make the call.

'Hi. Sorry it's a bit late.'

In times past, it might have been garnished with "babe," but I haven't ventured back there yet.

'I was thinking you might call. How did your day go?'

'Hell, actually.'

I summarize, opting to spare her the whole convoluted chain of events. I avoid the possibility of foul play at this point. It's best to build up to that.

Even so, she's practically in shock. 'Good God, Sebastian, you've been put through the wringer!'

It seems my summary doesn't do enough for her. She's full of questions. They take at least a half-hour. Thankfully, there's A Tale of Spices running parallel through to the end.

I put down the empty glass and recork the bottle. 'Needless to say, I'm left wondering if anyone among the five of them has reason to want Richard dead.'

'You mean murder!?'

'Speculation, at this point, that needs intensive investigation.'

'Your PI genes have been fully activated. I'm not surprised.'

'You could say that.'

'It sounds like you only have tomorrow,' she says.

'Right again.'

'Wish I could be a fly on the wall, watching you operate.'

'I'll miss having you around.' I wring up the courage. 'I guess there's not a chance you could drive out for the day?'

'Sorry.'

Quicker than expected.

'Really? You'd be invaluable.'

Silence . . . Still and all, dispiriting.

It's the first time I've broached the subject of joining investigative forces again, were I to find myself with another case on my hands.

'Sleep on it,' I say.

'I'll do that much.'

Not promising.

I know better than to press it any further—and risk crashing out entirely. 'I could use some sleep myself.' A rather lame signal that it's best to bring the call to an end.

'Good night then,' she says. 'I'll be thinking about you.'

''Night, babe.'

Who's willing to be the one to end the call? I think it better be me.

FIVE: WITLESS BAY

AS DESPERATE AS I am for it, I don't get much sleep. I have a mind in limbo, searching for a sense of how to stage-manage the day ahead.

Eyes jerked open by a knock on the door.

What the frig: 6:58 a.m. I haul back the covers, pull on pants and T-shirt.

Housekeeping? The RCMP? Not this early in the morning.

'My God, what are you doing here?'

'You're withdrawing your invitation?'

In walks Mae. Overnight bag in hand.

'I mean, holy crap, it's a surprise, that's all.'

'The manager gave me your room number.' We embrace, rather gracelessly. I push the door closed at the same time.

She sets the bag to one side and deposits her coat and gloves on top of it. 'I woke up thinking this is going to be more interesting than a day in the shop. Which in any event I would have had to close, given the forecast.'

'The forecast?'

'You haven't heard?'

'Other things on my mind.'

'We're in for a major dump of snow, starting later this morning. The whole of the east coast.'

'It's April.'

'It's Newfoundland.'

Of course she's right.

'They're saying it could break the record set in 2016.'

'Which was?

'Roughly 49.3 cm.'

'That's like almost two feet.'

Just when you start believing in spring, Mother Nature smacks you upside the head.

'You're here,' I tell her. 'That's terrific. We'll weather the storm together.'

'From what you described so far, there's more than one brewing.'

'That forecast is inconclusive. At this point, I'm just trying to get a handle on the atmospheric pressures.'

Too early in the morning. She shakes her head.

'No, really. We have an hour before breakfast. Let's just sit down, and I'll lay out the personalities in play, as much as I've been able to get a fix on them over the past couple of days. My take keeps changing. In any event, you'll be meeting all five at the same time, so you'll draw your own conclusions.'

My logic finds a home. She takes out the thermos of herbal tea she invariably travels with, pours an ex-whisky glass for each of us, and settles into the armchair. 'You're on.'

I pull on a pair of socks, haul a sweatshirt over my head, and settle into the chair opposite her. 'So. Here we go. Are you ready?'

She raises her glass and holds it in the air until I do the same. 'Into the wind.'

'The KNOT exec plus one.'

This is the ever-evolving take of Sebastian Synard. No fringe theories at this point. No loose conjecture or remote possibilities.

Carmel Ann Buttery. An off-centre powerhouse with ideas and the organizational skills to set them in motion. All the while retaining the level-headed control needed to deal with complications thrown her way. Comfortable in her own skin, but has gone through a lot to reach that point. Determined to shape a bright future, yet doesn't fit the picture of someone willing to go to extremes to get there.

Bobbie Freake. The woman behind the scenes who gets things done, yet determined, as far as her film career goes, to claim part of the spotlight, albeit in the dubious genre of horror-comedy. Easy going, up to a point. She realizes that, if her dream is to come true, the more decisive aspect of her nature must take hold. She also realizes she has limited time left to make it happen.

Tryphena Loveless. On the surface, dispassionate and near clinical in her approach to the world around her, yet surprising in the habits that give her particular pleasure. Has settled into a way of dealing with whatever it is that life has handed her—maintain a distance until such time that there's a job that needs to be done. Get it done, then withdraw to her private comforts.

Mort Coveyduck. Rural man of the world. Sociable, resourceful, clever in the practical sense. His years have left him with a solid understanding of outport life, which doesn't necessarily translate to the wider world. Yet his good nature usually wins out, no matter where he finds himself. He thrives on being charitable, but one suspects he has his prejudices.

Angelo Jones. Over the course of two days, the odd man out. Arrived with a flourish but may have grown tired of his role, accelerated by the demise of his rival. He is clearly anxious to fulfill his commitment and get out of Newfoundland. As much as the conference suited his purpose as a toponymist, he's become increasingly unnerved. It may have something to do with his meeting the person who paid the shot for his being here. Maybe. Maybe not.

'That would be the person by the name of Lonz Littlejohn?' says Mae.

'Correct.'

'Short for Alonzo, presumably?'

'Presumably, although odd for a kid from outport Newfoundland.'

'I would think. And you're not putting him in the mix of what you call "the personalities in play?"'

'As far as I saw, he had no direct contact with Richard Martin.'

'Yet he had a major stake in the conference and its outcomes.'

'True. I wasn't dismissing him,' I say. 'It's just that he's not someone you're about to meet at the breakfast table.'

'Nevertheless.'

'Fine. Add him to the list.'

Lonz Littlejohn. Royal pain in the butt. Has done very well for himself if you're a fan of movies that can make you laugh and scare the shit out of you at the same time. He's generous with his money, but it comes with a price. He's all about boosting his own profitability and will use any means, no matter how blatantly boorish, to get his own way. That said, he has his base of supporters more than willing to cheer him on.

'Whoa. You're not a fan, I take it.'

'Enough said. Breakfast calls. Time to take your seat at the table and start drawing your own conclusions.'

'I'm not sure how to handle this,' she says.

'No pressure. They're generally a friendly lot. In any case, the meal itself gives us lots to talk about.'

The dining room has been returned to its original purpose. Me strolling into it with Mae turns the heads of all four seated at the two adjoining tables set out for breakfast.

Mort, the fifth, who is just about to sit down, says what's on all their minds. 'Well now, isn't this a surprise. Sebastian, you're very good at keeping secrets.'

'Let me introduce Mae, my partner. She drove out this morning from St. John's. I hope you don't mind if she joins us for breakfast.'

'Absolutely not,' says Carmel Ann. Like the others, she is good at covering up the fact she's a little taken aback that someone new is joining the group, someone who had not been part of the drama that continues to consume its members. 'Please, take a seat.'

There is only one empty seat left. It appears that Jeanine, when she set the table at least, was unaware of what had transpired last evening. The one seat would have been occupied by Richard Martin. Mae sits down tentatively, the scenario having dawned on her.

Awkward silence is waiting to be filled. No one is bold enough to look directly at me, but I feel the scrutiny nonetheless.

'Mae owns and operates a fabric shop in St. John's that caters especially to quilters. She has business in this area, so she left early and stopped by to see me.'

All true, considering that the business has not been specified. I smile across the table at Mae, in appreciation of just how good it was of her to take the time to pay me a visit.

'There's lots of quilters up and down this shore,' notes Mort. 'What business exactly, if you don't mind me asking.'

I do mind. As a matter of fact, Mort, it's a business that's none of yours.

Mae is less perturbed. 'I conduct quilting workshops.'

'Oh, I see,' says Mort.

What he doesn't see is that she conducts them exclusively at her shop in St. John's. What he doesn't see is that Mae sailed deftly past his question.

Bobbie looks like she's about to ask one of her own.

'Touten, anyone?' I have the plate of toutens in my hand, holding it for those to the right of me. They dutifully fork the new focus of conversation onto their plates. And now a switch to those to the left. 'Don't forget the molasses.'

The touten plays such a useful role at the breakfast table. It brings all their attention to bear on that simple wad of fried bread dough.

'A beast of a Newfoundland culinary treat.' I could go on and on about the touten.

'Really, Sebastian,' says a suddenly scowling Angelo. 'We've been down that road before. Who gives a fuck?'

Carmel Ann nearly chokes. Mort makes a bizarre groaning sound. The rest of us, at the least, cease chewing for a few seconds.

Well now, isn't that a bit of a thunderclap. One for which it seems Angelo has no regrets. And which needs some sort of response on my part.

'Very well.'

Honestly, I can't come up with much else. And it appears that Angelo is not about to deal with the awkwardness in any way. He pushes his untouched touten to one side and fills the vacant section of his plate with a wedge of quiche.

'Fruit salad, anyone?' Bobbie holds up the bowl, offering to pass it along.

No takers. Which I take as a subtle rejection of Angelo's outburst. The rest of us continue savouring the toutens. I, for one, take a second, with an extra pour of molasses.

I glance in Mae's direction. Her eyes are noticeably wider. Her analytical mind is in high gear. What to make of Angelo? What to make of the silence around the table?

I don't feel it incumbent on me to take another stab at initiating conversation, even though the table is teeming with topics in need of attention. I look over at Carmel Ann—the president who, in the past, has been more than eager to step into the lead.

My eye catches hers. She's feeling the pressure. She finishes her touten and sets her fork and knife neatly across her plate.

She settles on an opening line. 'We are now in a position to make some decisions.'

As if we weren't before? It's as if new options have suddenly revealed themselves. I don't think so.

'As we are all aware,' Carmel Ann says, 'Staff Sergeant Larkin expects us to remain here at the inn until the results of the autopsy are known. Regardless of the results, he has further questions, and—in due course—will be in touch with me to arrange a time to interview each of us.'

'In due course,' snaps Angelo. 'What the fuck.'

Carmel Ann ignores his second outburst as she did the first, despite the fact he's staring resolutely at her.

'Which brings me to a second matter to be addressed. Namely, the Grand Tour, meant to start tomorrow. Given the travel restrictions, and the fact that the person who would have been a key member of our group is no longer with us, I am recommending the Grand Tour be cancelled.'

'As soon as the cops give us the go-ahead, we get the hell out of here,' declares Angelo.

It takes Mort, the treasurer, to raise the issue that must now be on the minds of all four of the KNOT exec. 'In which case we would need to make some adjustments to your contract, Mr. Jones.'

'The exercise that I agreed to undertake has been cancelled. What do you suggest I do—sit around for four days staring at you? And eat fucking toutens?'

The man is obsessed. (And his ruthless attack on the innocent touten totally without cause.)

It's got to be a front. Angelo Jones is diverting attention from the real questions. Why does he want out of here so quickly? What's he running away from?

Not something I'm about to raise, of course, but bravo to Mort for taking him on. Jones is under contract with KNOT for several days following the conference. Presumably KNOT will come up with a replacement for the Grand Tour. Whatever that might be.

Phoney though it is, Carmel Ann exudes a passive exterior. 'Following breakfast, the executive of KNOT will meet to formulate a plan to move forward. I ask for your understanding, and your continued respect for the memory of Richard Martin, a man of many fine qualities.'

'And a great admirer of the touten,' I add.

It's the last word on the subject. In fact, few words are uttered during the remainder of the meal. Angelo's hysterics hang like a black cloud over the moose sausages and partridgeberry muffins.

Only one thing breaks the lull—the crackling sound against the bank of windows.

'Sure sounds like ice pellets,' says Mort.

'Really?' says Carmel Ann.

Bobbie wins the smartphone race. 'You're kidding! Turning to snow. Forty-plus centimetres.'

'Not today. Not us.'

'That's what it says. The whole of the Avalon. Starting early morning on the Bonavista Peninsula, making its way south, all day and overnight. Upwards of forty-plus centimetres.'

'Good God.'

That pretty well sums it up. As I said, as months go in Newfoundland, April is wacko.

'Looks like nobody's going anywhere,' Mort says, with what could be taken as a note of satisfaction. He's lived through it all before.

Angelo, needless to say, is in a sweat. He's unwilling to give in to the weather, which is not a trait that does you any good in Newfoundland. I sense an expletive any second. Instead, he pushes back from the table and storms out of the dining room, presumably to seethe in his room.

Suddenly, despite the forecast, the black cloud has been lifted. The table is alive again with conversation.

In the midst of which, Mae excuses herself to make a phone call. She returns quickly and announces, 'The workshop has been cancelled. Nobody is willing to take a chance on getting caught in a snowstorm.'

Understandable, everyone agrees. 'Like I said, nobody's going anywhere,' adds Mort, with a measure of cockiness nobody understands.

Mae has my sympathy—and admiration for her clever manoeuvre. 'You can't be taking any chances yourself,' I tell her. 'In which case you'll just have to hang out with us until it's safe to head back to town.'

'Absolutely.' Good old Mort once again.

The chatter resumes. Eventually Carmel Ann breaks through it. 'Call to order. Call to order. I propose we consider this a formal meeting of the executive, together with Sebastian and Mae. Given his tour experience, Sebastian may have suggestions about how we make the best use of our time. In keeping with our mandate, if that is possible.'

It's apparent nobody quite knows what they're about, yet they do seem somewhat eager to press ahead and make the best of a disruptive situation.

'I therefore throw it open to the floor for suggestions,' declares Carmel Ann. 'Let's hear each of your thoughts on just what activities we could undertake that will make for a productive time together.'

They're very slow off the mark. A lot of figurative head-scratching.

Finally, Mort (no surprise) has an offering. 'How about charades? I'll pick say twenty-five Newfoundland and Labrador place names and throw them in a hat. The rest of you divide into two teams, I pass around the hat, each of you take a turn choosing one and acting it out. I'll keep time with a stopwatch, and the team with the fastest overall time wins!'

Well now, isn't that just going to take our minds off poor Richard stretched out on a slab in a morgue undergoing an autopsy. Really, Mort, that's blatantly tactless, to put it mildly.

'Count me out,' declares Tryphena, which amounts to the first thing she's said since Mae and I sat down.

'You're welcome to come up with something better,' counters Mort. 'We're all ears, Triffie.'

Mort's sarcastic, combative tone hikes the stress level. It undercuts Carmel Ann and sets Tryphena on the defensive.

'I don't know if you realize it, Mortimer,' Tryphena says coldly, 'but sometimes you haven't got a clue.'

Mort stiffens. He's not used to being seen as anything but a capable, easygoing asset to a discussion.

'Aren't you the charmer?' he manages, swallowing his disbelief.

'Now, now everyone, let's not get carried away.' It's Carmel Ann's attempt to get past her own disbelief. 'Our priority is to make the best of a difficult situation.'

'I have a suggestion,' says Bobbie. 'That is, if Mae and Sebastian are able to accommodate us. I'm wondering if they might be willing to give us an overview of the craft movement in Newfoundland.'

'Excellent suggestion, Bobbie,' announces Carmel Ann, desperate to turn the tide.

Before Mae and I have a chance to think about it, let alone respond, Mort is ready with a monkey wrench, clearly retribution for his own failed suggestion. 'That has absolutely nothing to do with our mandate,' he declares.

'I have zero interest in quilting,' says Tryphena, who looks to be in a particularly bad mood. 'Or rug hooking for that matter. As far as I'm concerned, knitting would be a waste of my time.'

The charmer is right.

Add Bobbie to the list of the offended. That makes all three of them at odds with each other.

It's an ill wind that blows nobody good. It won't be pleasant, but impulsive conflict between suspects has the potential to deliver serious clues as to who might be directly involved in a victim's demise.

It's the opportunity I've been hoping for. Here goes.

'May *I* offer a suggestion?'

They're looking at me as an unbiased outsider. Someone who is not a stakeholder in KNOT but presumably has their best interests at heart.

'Yes, please do,' says their president. She takes a deep breath. She's going to need it.

'My advice, considering we have limited time before Staff Sergeant Larkin shows up, is to focus on our witness statements. This is serious business. Remember, according to the RCMP, we're talking a potential crime scene.'

'That's cop talk,' says Bobbie. 'They're playing it safe. It's what they do. It's their job.'

'That's being optimistic,' I say.

'Surely the RCMP are not thinking any one of us . . . ' The thought appears to jolt Carmel Ann into alarmed silence.

'We *answered* his questions,' says Bobbie.

'Larkin didn't get the answers he was looking for. He wants details. What exactly was the relationship, if any, of each of us to Richard Martin.'

'Relationship?' injects Mort. 'What are you talking about? The man was here to speak to our conference. There was no relationship.'

'The RCMP are not into blanket responses,' I tell them. 'They deal in individuals.'

Another reality check. I sense their stress levels spiking.

I look around the table at an exec struggling to cope. To judge by her pallid, shocked expression, Tryphena, in particular, is having a tough time of it.

Only when my eye catches hers does her look change. 'You're some kind of expert?' she mutters.

I had been hoping it wouldn't get to this point.

'You work with the cops?' she adds. No louder, but heard by everyone around the table.

There's no avoiding it. Even so, it's better to reveal it now than have it come out at some point down the road and leave them thinking I've been playing a con game.

'In my other job, I have regular contact with the police.'

'Your other job?' says Carmel Ann.

'I'm a certified private detective. I work principally in the off-season, when the weather means tour guiding is not an option.'

'And here he is, in exactly that situation,' Mae notes, directing her hand toward the bank of windows. The ice pellets have now turned to snow, obstructing the view. If it's her attempt to inject a little humour, it falls flat.

The KNOT exec had no idea. I guess because not one of them has had any interest in googling my name. If they had, they would have seen reference to more than one of the cases that have hit the news in the past.

Their stress levels appear to have risen another few notches.

'So now you're doing double duty,' Mort says pointedly.

'Or you've switched roles altogether,' asserts Bobbie, 'since you're guiding us absolutely nowhere.'

Their delivery borders on aggressive. Not what I hoped for.

I better nip that in the bud before it gets more oxygen.

'Remember, I'm square in the middle of what happened to Richard as much as any of you are. Each of us is what cops call "a person of interest." We're all in this together.'

No one disagrees. I need to shore up that position even more.

'Let's face it, who in their right mind would think an organization would arrange for a guest speaker, then plot to have him killed? All I want to do is prepare you for dealing with the RCMP. The more thorough our witness statements, the quicker they'll be done with us.'

There's the story. Enough to win back their trust. I hope. At one level, I'm their confidante, their knowledgeable advisor. At the other, I'm their covert watchdog, my PI radar compiling mental notes on just who among them might have had a motive for harming Richard.

You could call it a con game of sorts. Or subterfuge, to sound a bit more rational. I go with *tactful plan of action*.

I glance at Mae, sensing she's starting to feel a little uncomfortable, a hanger-on with nothing worthwhile to contribute.

Of course, she can't say or do anything that would even hint at the fact she had a pivotal role in my last three investigations. But rather than playing the fabric-shop owner with time on her hands, I'm thinking there's a way she could be doing a tactful bit of investigative business of her own.

'Mae and I have an acquaintance who is an inspector with the Royal Newfoundland Constabulary. Mae, you'll remember we had a lengthy discussion with him at one point about witness statements.'

That would be Olsen, live-in of my ex, Samantha. Although we've all spent time together—as strained as it has been at times—reference to the topic of witness statements is stretching it.

'Mae, would you be willing to highlight what the police expect in such a statement, and perhaps assist anyone who might need help formulating their own?'

Of course she would. She's caught the ball and is about to run with it. 'I'd be more than happy to help out in any way I can. Inspector Olsen had such a thorough knowledge of the subject.'

I'm waiting for at least one of them to buy into the offer. I sense raw skepticism. I sweep the table with an encouraging smile.

'A good suggestion, Sebastian. Thank you,' says Carmel Ann, finally.

A tad underwhelming, but it serves the purpose. The woman is desperate to move things along.

I'm prepared to do just that. 'Let's move to the sofas, shall we? And relax with our coffee and tea.'

They make the move reluctantly, their suspicions only partially quelled. I use the pause in the action to make a quick trip to retrieve my laptop, and so Mae can make a trip to her car for pens and notepads.

On the way back from my room, I knock soundly on Angelo's door. 'We need you in the seating area. We're having a crack at our witness statements.' I don't expect an answer. I move on.

Back at the sofas, it's a broody exec. Only Mae and Carmel Ann are conversing. The other three, despite sitting inches from each other, prefer to seethe in the resentment that flared during breakfast.

I take a chair from the dining area and seat myself slightly apart from the sofas, establishing a little breathing room to take the lead. Besides, it leaves a spot for Angelo, should he make up his volatile mind to join us.

Speak of the devil. In he strides and planks himself down on the sofa, in the gap between Tryphena and Bobbie. It happens so abruptly that none of the others know how to react.

I plunge in before they do, as Mae hands out pens and notepads both bearing the charming logo of her fabric store. 'Well, folks. Let's consider this an information session.' I look over at Angelo. 'Both Mae and I have had occasion to compose witness statements for the police. Based on our first-hand experience and our additional conversation with Inspector Frederick Olsen, we feel we can be useful in pinpointing the elements that the RCMP will be looking for in your respective submissions.'

'Exactly what "first-hand experience"?' Angelo says, eager to make his presence felt.

Although I'd prefer to avoid the backstory, there's no choice but to give at least a nominal version. 'On a beach we came upon the body of a young man who had drowned. As it turned out, foul play was suspected.'

I avoid the *M* word. The mood is taut enough as it is. The quicker we get past this the better.

'Murdered?' retorts Angelo.

The dear man. Thank you. I shouldn't be surprised, given the Memphis homicide stats.

'Yes,' I say. That's all he's getting.

'Drugs?' inserts Mort. 'Ten to one there were drugs involved.' All eyes are now fixed in my direction.

'Yes.' That's all they're getting. 'As I was saying, the question is, what exactly does the Royal Canadian Mounted Police expect of a witness statement? Mae and I will create a list, and when it's complete, we'll forward it to your inboxes. I open a new screen and begin typing as I speak, slowly, allowing my untrained fingers time to catch up.

'Number one: Your full name, date and place of birth, citizenship, permanent residence. Contact information: mailing address, telephone, email.'

'Obviously,' says Angelo.

I let it pass. 'Number two: Indicate where you were at the time of the incident, and why exactly you were there.'

Mae steps in. 'Let me stress that the officers in charge of the investigation will be looking for details. What led you to be part of the conference? Where were you situated during the course of the evening, and why that particular location?'

'We told him that already,' says Bobbie.

'But you haven't sworn to it,' I counter. 'This will be a sworn written statement.'

'Potential evidence in a court of law,' adds Mae.

Unavoidably blunt, unfortunately. Stress on top of stress.

'You're making it sound like we're a bunch of criminals,' Mort said.

Damn it all, Mort. You're not that dense.

'Innocent until proven guilty,' pipes up Bobbie.

Dear God.

I try to rein them in. 'You're getting carried away. This is simply a witness statement, a record of what you personally experienced in relation to the incident. That's it. Period.'

'Face it, Synard,' snaps Angelo, 'if there was fucking foul play, we're all suspects. Call a spade a fucking spade.'

Whoa. Try smacking me up against a wall, why don't you? Jesus.

Dead silence while I figure out how to deal with the bugger.

Mort gets there before me. 'In your experience as a private detective . . . '

'He's a PI?!' thunders Angelo. 'What the fuck is going on?'

Good question.

To make a long, ill-humoured story short, the attempt to return to the witness-statement prep session disintegrates into a shouting match. Angelo's the loudest, but a couple of others giving him a run for his money. Mae and I extricate ourselves. I close the laptop.

Carmel Ann is on the verge of tears. 'Please, please, PLEASE . . . '

Something that finally brings them to their senses. For a few moments, there's near silence.

'You Canadians are so goddamn polite,' mutters Angelo, sarcastic ass, out to have the final word.

With it, he abruptly exits once again, doing us all a favour.

Should I reopen the laptop? There's no point. The atmosphere has been permanently fouled.

Carmel Ann has a hand against her forehead, her eyes closed.

'Are you okay?'

'Migraine.'

I look at the others disapprovingly. 'Let's give Carmel Ann some peace and quiet. For a change.'

The looks I get in return amount to, *Who exactly put you in charge?*

To be blunt, someone needs to show some common sense, and it doesn't look like it's going be any one of the three individuals staring my way.

'If I were you, I'd find someplace to write your statements. If anyone has questions, Mae and I are here to answer them.'

In the meantime, Carmel Ann's head rests awkwardly against the back of the sofa, her eyes still closed. Mae helps her change positions so she's lying the length of the sofa, requiring Mort to vacate it. Which he promptly does, coming to land on the opposite sofa in the spot left by Angelo, between the equally resentful Bobbie and Tryphena.

Both women launch themselves upright, as if Mort's impact had triggered springs in the sofa that propelled them to their feet. With that they head off in separate directions, Bobbie to one of the vacant dining-room tables, and Tryphena to her room, presumably.

Mort is left to his own devices, which for the moment amounts to peering out the nearest window with what looks to be increasing excitement at the sight of snow obscuring the view. The misfit relishes the notion of a pending winter storm, even in April. Anything to add to his stockpile of stories, ripe for the retelling.

Mae and I need privacy. The only place we're certain not to be overheard is in my room.

Now our room. While I take to an armchair and flounder in the effort to relax, Mae unpacks her overnight case.

I vent when she finishes. 'What the hell? If you were to pick someone who gave the slightest hint that he or she had a grudge against Richard, who would you pick?'

Mae takes to the other chair. 'Tryphena.'

I'm amazed she responded so quickly. 'For real? She hardly said a word.'

'That's just it—why? Why was she so reluctant to get involved?'

'Could be her nature? Tryphena looked uncomfortable. Could be she's intimidated by how the tempers flared.'

'Have you had conversations with her?'

I think back over the last couple of days. 'One. When I first arrived, before the conference started. We talked about whisky and books.'

It sparks Mae's interest big time. I relate as much of the conversation as I can recollect.

'Didn't it strike you as odd?' she says. 'I mean . . .'

'I didn't ask. It didn't occur to me at the time. I thought it was just coincidence.'

'And what piece of solo fiction did she recommend?'

'Actually, she didn't. She didn't get back to me.'

'And you didn't remind her?' Mae asks.

'To be honest, once the conference began, I didn't see much of her.'

'You think she was avoiding you?'

'I just figured she was busy,' I tell her. 'In the kitchen, directing the catering.'

'Which is another reason she's worked her way to the top of my list. Of all of them, she's the only one who had ready access to Richard's meal.'

Obviously, that struck me as soon as the cops first uttered

the words "potential crime scene."

'So the question becomes, just what do we do with that tidy little fact?'

'Say she did contaminate the meal,' Mae says. 'Is there any possibility that traces of the contaminant remain?'

'You mean in the kitchen in Stagehead? I doubt it very much. If there was anything left on Richard's plate, it would have been dumped with the scraps from every other plate, and then his plate washed clean. I suspect the counters would all have been scoured even before the Mounties showed up. In any case, the kitchen has been locked and won't be touched by anyone but a forensics squad, should one be called in.'

'I wasn't thinking only the kitchen,' Mae says.

'Where else?'

'Was she carrying anything when you all drove back to the inn last evening, like a tote bag?'

'Probably. The exec always seems to be toting something or other.'

'Then let's say there was something in the bag, say a vial with traces of the contaminant.'

I go along with that. I'm not about to burst Mae's bubble. Not that I necessarily think it's likely.

'I know what you're thinking,' she says. 'Why bring back the vial? Why not dispose of it once the RCMP showed up?'

'Maybe too many people in the kitchen for someone not to notice. And even if no one did, it still would be found if the cops did a thorough search.'

'Exactly.'

'In which case it might still be in her room.' Or, which I don't add, crushed and flushed down the toilet.

'The quicker we get into her room and search it the better.'

Right. At the very least, Mae's logic has hit a brick wall. I resist the urge to be that blunt.

'Just how do we get her out of the room, without her locking the door behind her? And get her far enough away that one of us can slip inside unnoticed?'

Took the words right out of my mouth.

Mae answers her own questions. 'Teamwork.'

A heartening word, but one fraught with more unanswered questions.

'You come up with something that gets her out of the room while I slip inside,' Mae says. 'Or vice versa.'

Need I point out the glaring lack of detail? No. Such an investigative opportunity can't be ignored.

Yet as someone once said, "It's the little details that are vital. Little things make big things happen." If I recall correctly, an American college basketball coach talking about the game of life. Despite such questionable credentials, he had a point.

Fifteen minutes later, it's time for the jumpshot. Let the game begin.

Gentle knock on Tryphena's door.

Mae: 'Triffie, have you got a moment?'

Tryphena opens the door.

Mae: 'Would you mind? Sebastian has asked me to look into the possibilities for lunch. Given your catering background, I'm wondering if you would come to the kitchen with me and offer a few suggestions as to what might make a meal. The inn, as you know, only does breakfast. Jeanine has finished up for the day, but she did say that, under the circumstances, we're welcome to whatever we can find.'

Triffie: 'Oh.'

Mae: 'I know it's an imposition. But it won't take long.'

Triffie: 'I guess so.'

Mae: 'Wonderful. Thanks so much.'

Triffie: 'Wait while I get my key.'

Mae: 'Don't bother. It'll only take a minute or two.'

Three minutes, thirteen seconds actually. As it turns out, time enough for me to catch a glimpse of them rounding the corner on the way to the kitchen as I slip into Tryphena's room and plunge into action. I've had experience at this.

The prime object of interest sits in an armchair. I rifle through it carefully, by touch alone, extracting the one thing that holds any promise. It turns out to be mascara in a tube. The tote bag is a waste of thirty seconds.

The bathroom also proves a dud. I lose valuable seconds examining the array of tubes and jars lining the glass shelf above the sink. Likewise, giving the once-over to the clothes in the dresser drawers gets me nowhere except vaguely embarrassed.

The overnight case is the last hope. I grab it from the closet, fumbling to open it, cursing the time wasted on the expansion zipper. It's stuffed with dirty clothes. Except for a bulge in a side pocket.

Inside is a small blue canister labelled with what looks to be Japanese script. Or Chinese, or Korean. I turn it around to the opposite side. Also indecipherable. I snap two quick pictures with my phone, replace the canister, zip up the case, set it back in the closet, and slip back into the corridor, shutting the door behind me.

I hear Mae's voice. Something about eggs. Loud enough that it's her warning me to get my ass back into our room. I check the time. Three minutes, three seconds.

Ten seconds later, our room door opens.

'So what's for lunch?'

Mae closes the door behind her, briefly amused. 'Not a lot. Toast and scrambled eggs.'

'Tryphena could liven it up with a little seafood seasoning?'

I hold up my phone. Mae draws closer to the screenshot of the photo I sent through the translation app.

'" . . . an all-purpose seasoning with plenty of seafood

flavour based on fresh shrimp-head extract, clams, kelp, oysters, etc. Use it to flavour assorted dishes. It's as good as your imagination."'

Mae slumps into the other chair, overawed. 'Send me the original shots.'

'Something's shellfishy. Agreed?'

Several minutes on our laptops confirm that yes, absolutely, shellfish protein in seasoning powder—even trace amounts—could easily trigger an allergic reaction.

'The most common culprit is a muscle protein called *tropomyosin*,' Mae says, 'found in both crustaceans and mollusks.'

'A toponymist done in by tropomyosin,' I observe.

Not an attempt at humour. It merely caught my attention. Neither one of us is smiling.

In fact, it's a rather sad conclusion. If indeed Tryphena purposely contaminated the sauce that covered the stuffed chicken breast.

'If she did, what was the motive? I can't believe it was merely because she didn't agree with Richard's take on place names.'

Mae's right. 'There has to be more to it. For starters, we need a background check on the woman.'

Some of which we can do ourselves by searching online. And possibly by dropping a few questions to other members of the exec. Although that has severe limitations, since we can't be raising suspicions about what we're up to. Being sequestered in an inn in Dildo has definite disadvantages.

'You could call Frederick,' Mae says. 'When it comes to reports of criminal behaviour, he'd have ready access even if no charges were laid.'

'I could.' Not that I want to.

The abruptness of my reply says it all. I hate having to rely on my ex-wife's RNC stud, except when there's no way around it.

'I thought you were over that.'

Obviously, Mae thinks I should be. We won't go there.

'Let's see what we come up with,' I say.

After an exhaustive search of the internet, nothing. As might be expected, there are very few people in the world named Tryphena (or Triffie, or Trif) Loveless. Those that reveal themselves can be counted on two fingers. One is a retired gamekeeper in Australia; the other died in 1897. If our Tryphena was gainfully employed by a company, the internet is not eager to reveal it. As for her social media profile, it's non-existent.

In other words, I make the call. 'Hey, Frederick, how's it goin'?'

'Not bad. Yourself? I understand from Nick you're involved in a peculiar conference of some kind.'

'You could say that.'

I make the leap into the chronicle of what transpired last evening. I stop there. There's no need to get into details that would get Frederick thinking I'm on to something better left in the hands of the RCMP.

'So possible foul play. Right up your alley. You've switched roles, I take it.'

'You could say that.'

'What's the person's name, and what do you need to find out?'

Does it sound like we've been through this scenario before? That would be the case. The last time less than a year ago.

I deliver the name and its variations. I suspect Frederick's smiling.

'Definitely no chance of there being more than one person with that name,' he says. 'I take it you're interested in knowing if she shows up in court records.'

'That would be the case.'

'It's Monday morning. I'm up to my eyeballs. Give me a couple of hours.'

'Thanks.'

That's the extent of the conversation. I generally avoid small talk with Frederick. It tends to put extra strain on our interpersonal relationship.

In the interim, there's time to put another of our investigative strategies in play. 'Let's get out there and discreetly engage with the troops. Let's see what they know about Triffie.'

Mae volunteers to take on Mort. As we've seen, he's been referred to by his colleague Triffie as "clueless." Mae thinks he just might be willing to vent.

I'm game to have a go at Carmel Ann, whose frustration at the clash of personalities this morning might just make her willing to point fingers. I find her in the kitchen making herself a cup of coffee.

'This is my third,' she says. Not a good sign if she's trying to calm her nerves although it might help with her migraine. Either way, it could play to my advantage.

'May I join you?'

'I could use the company.'

Promising. I select a Kicking Horse Kick Ass dark-roast pod and set it in the machine.

We take to stools on opposite sides of the kitchen's island. Carmel Ann appears as anxious as I am to have her frustrations flow.

She takes a deep breath, exhaling loudly. 'I can't believe the infighting. There's no need. They could at least have stayed level-headed through all this.'

Her mind is overloaded. She welcomes a sounding board. Someone with no reason to repeat what she says.

As luck would have it, I'm her man.

'They're stressed,' I tell her. Not to defend them. More to see where it leads. 'They ended up saying things they don't really mean. Like Triffie telling Mort he doesn't have a clue.'

I'm smiling, she's not. 'Triffie surprised me.'

'She's not herself,' Carmel Ann says.

Whatever "herself" might have been. 'How did she get involved in KNOT?'

'She's a relative newcomer. She didn't join until after we had done most of the planning for the conference. We were at the point of deciding on the food and drink requirements. Triffie ran a catering company once, so I jumped at her offer to help out.'

'Where was the company?'

'St. John's.'

'Did she tell you the name? I might have it heard of it. Mae uses caterers for special events at her shop.' (Well, once at least.)

'Not that I remember. She did say it specialized in seafood.'

Really. Sounds like a strategy to sell herself to Carmel Ann.

'She was very helpful when we were planning the menu for the banquet. As you heard me say, I was personally in favour of pan-fried cod. Triffie convinced us that various types of shellfish would be a more interesting option.'

'Was that before or after you learned that Richard was allergic to shellfish?'

'After. Triffie assured us that she could serve an alternate meal. Said she had to do it all the time when running her business. It was common practice.'

'I see.' That's not all I see. 'Triffie doesn't strike me as someone who ran a catering company. Having to deal with the public . . . I wouldn't think it's anything she'd enjoy. To me she's an introvert, don't you think?'

Carmel Ann takes a moment. 'She warned me she wouldn't have any time to take part in the conference sessions if that's what you're thinking. She had to be working behind the scenes, in the kitchens. Being in charge of all the food was a big commitment.'

Reason enough not to be seen in the audience, on either day of the conference.

With that thought, my chat with Carmel Ann comes to an abrupt end.

'What's happening with lunch? I'm starved.' It's Angelo, showing up as if he hadn't stormed off in a rage earlier—twice at that.

I can't resist. 'Are you good with scrambled eggs and toast? And juice. And of course, coffee. Lots of coffee.'

'Breakfast all over again. No, thank you.'

It's another blow to Carmel Ann, just when she was getting a grip on herself.

I put it to him. 'What do you suggest, Angelo? The inn only serves breakfast. We don't exactly have much choice.'

'Eat out, obviously.'

'Have you looked outside? I doubt if anything is open.'

'Call and find out. Isn't that the logical thing to do?'

Such a gem of a man.

Nevertheless, Carmel Ann is on her phone. To the two places within short driving distance, possibly reachable through driving snow.

The closest—the restaurant at Dildo Brewing Co. Quick to answer. Just as quick to say, 'Sorry, we're about to close. Our staff needs to get home before the storm gets any worse.'

A little further away—Dildo Coffee House. Also quick to answer. Closing in an hour.

Carmel Ann looks at me. 'Think you can make it?'

'Of course we can make it,' injects Angelo. 'Don't tell me you Newfoundlanders are phobic about a little snow. I read online that some years you get 150 inches or more.'

Oh, just shut the frig up, why don't you? Besides, when it comes to snow, we don't deal in inches. We're metric, you dickhead.

Thinking it, not saying it. '*We Newfoundlanders* can handle anything.'

Regardless, Carmel Ann gives in to him, on the condition the others in the group agree. Angelo goes in pursuit of them.

He's not about to take no for an answer.

SIX: BLOW ME DOWN

WE'RE ALL BUNDLED in as much winter gear as we thought we would need for April. Not a heck of a lot, but enough to get us out the door and to the van.

We face a white Mercedes hunkered under a mass of snow, with more swirling about it all the time. Ethereal, and a pain in the butt. Mae, Mort, and myself, together with a single scraper dug from the glove box, clear away the snow as best we can, with the others tucked inside the van, including the hooded, leather-gloved instigator of this whole senseless venture.

With the wipers going mad, I gun the Sprinter through the drifts and out of the parking lot.

The road is no better. Worse, in fact. It hasn't been plowed.

'It won't be until the storm is over,' says the zealous Mort. He's in the passenger seat, leaning forward, as close to the windshield as his seat belt will allow.

The visibility is worsening by the minute. I can barely make out the tire tracks heading in the opposite direction. There's no choice but to take it slow, with the assumption we won't end up in a ditch. Thankfully, it's a straight stretch of road, past the Dildo brewery and its empty, snow-covered parking lot.

At that point, no more tire tracks. Obviously, the tracks that were helping me navigate the road came from staff of the brewery heading home.

We haven't gone much further when Mort announces, 'Right turn where the sign says Hill Road.'

What sign? The sign we can't make out through the wall of swirling snow. That one? I turn anyway, on Mort's cue.

Hill Road? What the hell. The last thing we need is an incline.

'I'm not sure this was such a good idea,' Carmel Ann pipes up from behind me.

I'll be more precise. It was a bloody piss-poor idea. My only hope is that the fellow who came up with it is shit baked.

'Not far now,' says Mort, in a failed attempt to offset the stress.

I touch the brakes. The van swerves slightly before the tires catch. Ice patches. Just what we need.

The Sprinter senses something is up. Damn it all, the Mercedes-Benz technology kicks in. It's acting like we've struck the Bavarian Alps. Slow and unswervingly steady.

Mort urges her on, rocking forward in his seat. 'Yes, that's it, yes.'

I'm driving uphill through what's turned into a blizzard, but we'll get there if it kills me.

'Just before All Saints' Anglican Church, right turn onto Rube Reid's Lane,' Mort announces, sounding equally defiant.

Yes! Our prayers are answered. Right turn and back on the level. The Dildo Coffee House is just a straight assault over the snow-covered road.

'We made it!' yells Angelo, clapping his hands. 'I knew you could do it, Sebastian!'

Supercilious dickhead.

Five passengers file out amid a chorus of overcharged thanks. Off they trudge ahead of Mae and me, through the drifts and up the wheelchair ramp to the entrance, a skewed procession of storm-sapped survivors.

'Well, look at you folks!' The two staff of the empty coffee shop are as awestruck as we are. 'We were just about to give you up for stranded in a snow bank.'

'Only by the grace of God and Mercedes-Benz,' I say.

They, at least, laugh. As does Mae. Which is more than I can say for the rest of them.

'I'm Gavin and this is Francine. You have the pick of tables. Seat yourselves and I'll be right there with menus.'

Needless to say, the Dildo Coffee House is situated on a hill, with a bank of windows higher and broader than those of the inn. The view from the tables we join together to seat the seven of us is potentially spectacular, if for the moment all but obliterated by a slashing barrage of snow squalls.

'Too cozy for words,' says Mae. A miscalculation.

They're in the mood for food and nothing else.

On that level, at least, there's plenty to satisfy them. The piping hot turkey-vegetable soup, with grilled cheese on sourdough on the side, does the job very nicely. As does the smoked meat on a pretzel bun. For several fulfilling minutes, it takes my mind off the fact that I'll soon be reversing course and driving back through a blizzard.

The coffee, fittingly, is a brew called Gros Morne Dark Fog. To quote the roaster's words, it's "for those who are drawn to the darker end of the spectrum." That would be me at the moment, confirmed when I look around the table.

How dark? Angelo has turned obnoxiously dark. Although she wouldn't admit it, Tryphena is potentially pitch-black, depending on the results of the autopsy. As for Carmel Ann and Bobbie, they're in a twilight zone, navigating their way between gloom and doom. Even Mort looks about to fall victim to the collective angst.

I don't want to be dealing with this on the drive back. There's no need. They could use a pep talk. As a tour guide, it's in my job description.

'Hang in there. It could be a lot worse. The power lines could be down and you'd be surviving on corn flakes and apple juice. As my father used to say, "Keep your pecker up!"'

Mort suddenly rises from the doldrums. 'So did *my* father. A little snow never hurt anyone. Yes, by God, we'll all keep our peckers up!'

A rallying cry if there ever was one.

The foreigner among us has been decidedly left in the dark. By the look on his face and its reddish tint, Angelo has never heard the expression. Not only that, he finds it rather suggestive. Of an erection, one assumes.

'In Newfoundland we refer to a lovers' lane as a pecker's point,' I tell him.

'You're joking.'

Of course I am, dickhead, but I'm not about to admit to that. It's payback time for your tantrums this morning. Let's hope "pecker's point" turns up in your next speech as a world expert on toponymy.

Although Gavin and Francine don't say what's on their minds, I can see it's about time to close up shop so they can head home out of the storm.

'What say we pay up and face the elements, folks. Remember, as fathers in Newfoundland are prone to say . . . '

'Keep your pecker up!' Stiffly but somewhat in unison—except, of course, for Angelo.

Once we're actually in the great outdoors, it proves even more of a challenge than I was expecting. Unlike Gavin and Francine, who are within a short walking distance of their home turf, we're dealing with a vehicle that's again blanketed in snow and that's headed for a road more choked with the white stuff than when we arrived.

There's no time to spare. The survivors take to the inside of the Mercedes while the cleaning crew do a fast job on the windows. Then, doors closed, seat belts snapped, we're encased together, our obstructed sights set on the Come by the Bay Inn.

It's into a wall of white, broken only by glimpses of utility poles and the occasional house. They provide barely enough assurance that we're somewhere in the middle of Rube Reid's Lane and heading for the infamous Hill Road.

'All Saints ahead, left turn,' announces Mort.

I come to a stop at the intersection. 'Take a moment, everyone, and say a prayer.' Only half joking.

I make the left turn, away from the church. The hellish descent begins.

From what Mort and I recall, the hill veers slightly before descending straight down to where it meets the main road. Just how much it veers is the question, one with only a dubious answer since we've run out of houses to act as guideposts. We're left with only furtive utility poles and traces of the black cables strung between them. And, presumably, a ditch somewhere between us and the poles?

I have no intention of finding out. My aim is to maintain a constant distance between the Sprinter and the utility poles, under the assumption they have been erected at a consistent distance from the road.

There's one positive. I have no worries about encountering another vehicle coming up the road. There can't be another driver foolish enough to be out in this mess.

Slow and steady gets us to the base of the hill, as confirmed by Mort, who's lowered his window and declared, 'Stop, that's a street sign! We made it to the intersection.'

I've regained my bearings enough to know the shoreline of Dildo Harbour is dead ahead. From what I recall, there's a guardrail of sorts. The picture in my mind is of an ancient barrier about two feet high, made of decaying wood with zero structural integrity.

I make a laborious turn to the left. And continue my utility pole and cable strategy.

All well and good . . . for the few seconds before the storm ramps up even more. No less than a ten on the blizzard scale. What's visible beyond the windshield is absolutely nothing except a frantic pair of wipers doing bugger all to improve the situation.

I bring the Sprinter to a dead stop, hopefully on the road although I have no way of knowing for sure.

'Now what?' says Mort, unofficial spokesperson for the KNOT exec.

Mae leans forward from her seat directly behind me and whispers in my ear, 'They're *all* shit baked.'

After a few seconds staring through the windshield into the unrelenting wall of white, she looks back. 'Take our word for it, folks. There's no choice but to stay put until there's a break in the weather.'

'Sit back, relax,' Mort calls to them, sounding resentful that his position as the driver's confidant has been usurped. 'You can't argue with Mother Nature.'

'Mother Nature can go to hell,' retorts Angelo.

'Idiot!' shouts Mae. Through the blinding blizzard she's seen headlights, faint but unmistakable.

'Asshole!'

The headlights turn onto the road and are now heading straight for us! Below them, I see something broad and caustic yellow—a snowplow blade.

There's no choice but gun the Sprinter for all she's bloody worth!

I cut like mad to the right and out of its bloody way.

Just barely! Jesus. Mae grabs onto me.

I jam on the brakes. The van rams face-first into a snowbank and comes to a dead stop. Mercifully, the snow was light enough that the impact didn't deploy the airbags.

I find a breath and breathe again.

'Sweet mother of God,' mutters Mort, 'Talk about close. Some damn yahoo in a Dodge Ram. Doubt if he even saw us.'

The Sprinter is a ghost in a snowbank, but in one piece, its passengers severely rattled but nevertheless uninjured. Confirmed by the flood of sighs filling the space behind me.

Now the question is, just where the hell are we?

I force open the door, wide enough to wedge my upper body above its frame. Mort does the same on the passenger side. We can make out each other's bare head, though only just, across the expanse of the windshield. We nod single-mindedly.

Faces into the storm, we manage to discern the broad side of a building. Good God, we're marooned in the snowbank, one probably plowed up by that same idiot asshole, in the parking lot of the Dildo brewery.

There's no going ahead. The only way out of this is to back up onto the road.

Mort and I get back inside, and I try doing just that.

The Mercedes-Benz makes a valiant try but, in the end, decides it's had enough. Apparently no one told its engineers it would have to deal with a full-on Newfoundland blizzard and some damn yahoo in a Dodge Ram.

I turn to the traumatized faces behind me. 'We're stuck. We've reached the end of the road. There's no going any farther.'

'What the fuck.' No surprise where that originates. In recovery from being shit baked.

'The good news is we're within short walking distance of the inn.'

'And the bad news is we're not dressed for it,' says Angelo. 'Goddamn it all, I'm not going anywhere.'

'Fine! Goddamn it all, stay put. We'll be expecting you when the weather clears in the morning. By then you'll be half frozen. Not to mention bloody well starved. There'll be a stack of toutens on the breakfast table waiting for you.'

Mort is out of the van and sliding back the side door so the others can exit. 'More good news,' he tells them. 'The main road has had a cut with the snowplow. You won't be up to your knees in snow, only up to your ankles.'

No one is particularly relieved since there's a thigh-deep slog ahead of them to get from the van to the road.

Still, no one complains. They reach the road and trudge on in single file, each with a hand on the shoulder of the person ahead, in lockstep with Mort, who's in the lead and attempting, as he trudges, to clear a path for them by booting aside the snow.

Angelo hasn't moved. I slam the side door shut and follow the others, bringing up the rear.

It's a bizarre but inspiring sight—a trail of six Newfoundlanders heads into the fearsome wind and snow, determined to seize control of a miserable situation.

I feel a song coming on.

I inhale deeply and belt it out. *'We'll rant and we'll roar like true Newfoundlanders . . . '*

That's all it takes. An unflinching chorus of voices pounds into the blizzard.

'We'll rant and we'll roar on deck and below,
Until we strikes bottom inside the two sunkers,
When straight through the channel to Toslow we'll go.

I'm a son of a sea-cook, and a cook in a trader,
I can dance, I can sing, I can reef the main boom;
I can handle a jigger, and cuts a fine figure,
Whenever I gets in a boat's standing room.'

Third verse same as the first.

By God, we're a valiant crew, even if one of us is possibly a murderer.

It's no more than two hundred metres to the Come by the Bay Inn. We're still ranting and roaring when we turn into the driveway.

'We made it!' yells Mort, gathering his flock around him in celebration.

I'm about to give us all a rousing cheer when, looking back to the route we've just taken, I detect the likeness of a snow-battered human.

I'm stunned to see a sheep-like Angelo Jones take shape, plodding his way toward the inn. I pretend not to notice as he sidles into the driveway and stands apart from us all.

Then, as we head toward the guest entrance around the side of the inn, I'm stunned a second time.

Tracks, only partially snowed in, end in a bruiser of an RCMP truck whose tire treads could have scaled Hill Road like it was a one-horse race.

'A Ford F-250,' says an admiring Mort. White, but with added, attention-grabbing detail. Bold red, yellow, and blue body stripes. Hefty front bumper push bar. Potentially pulsating light bar.

Down from it step Staff Sergeant Larkin, Constable O'Rourke, and Constable Blanchett, all suitably attired in blizzard-proof parkas, undoubtedly thermal leather gloves, and the utterly classic fur hats. They are, of course, confounded to see us outside, sparingly dressed while subjecting ourselves to the elements.

'I wondered why no one answered the door,' Larkin yells into the wind. 'Or my phone calls.'

We were otherwise occupied. That aside, if he had undertaken the drive from Harbour Grace in this weather, he must have something deadly serious on his mind. Something requiring nothing less than our immediate, face-to-face attention.

It will, however, have to wait until we parade past the now unlocked door, free ourselves of our outdoor gear—such as it is—and warm up enough with hot tea or coffee that we can sit with some degree of comfort on the sofas in the seating area next to the dining room.

While the officers wait impatiently, I introduce them to Mae. They politely acknowledge her, although she's not what Larkin could call a "person of interest."

The head Mountie is nearing the end of his tether when Carmel Ann finally gives him the nod.

'I'm here to set you straight on what to expect of the next twenty-four hours,' he says.

Not a promising start. We're doubtless in for a seriously heavyweight announcement.

'I hope it's positive,' says Mort, who is clearly not good at reading body language.

'I was afraid of this,' says Angelo, who clearly is.

'There is nothing to be afraid of,' Larkin says. 'Let the police operation run its course, and everything will be dealt with in a timely manner.'

"Operation" sounds long and entangled. I brace myself.

'The autopsy report is now in my hands,' Larkin says.

Figuratively, of course. In any case, his eyes are our focus. They've grown markedly more intense. A pause accentuates the gravity of what is about to be revealed.

'Richard Martin died as a result of anaphylaxis, a severe allergic reaction. In this case, to a protein found in shellfish known as *tropomyosin*.'

I feel one step ahead of the game. The question now is, how did tropomyosin get into the meal he was served.

'The primary question from the standpoint of the RCMP,

of course, is how tropomyosin found its way into the meal served to Richard Martin.'

Two steps ahead of the game.

'Was it accidental? If it was, then how was that possible, given the precautions that were said to have been taken.'

There's a longish pause as the staff sergeant looks across at Carmel Ann and Tryphena, who happen to be sitting next to each other. Carmel Ann feels it is her duty to nod.

Larkin continues. 'If, on the other hand, it was deliberate, then . . . Though I hesitate in saying this—only because of its repercussions for anyone who was in the vicinity of the meal delivered to and consumed by Mr. Martin . . . If it was deliberate, then this could be considered a case of murder in the first degree.'

His final few words are nothing short of a bombshell.

Stunned silence. Everyone lashed with the same thought. In Larkin's eyes, are we all suspects? I glance at Tryphena. She's rigid.

The silence is broken, not surprisingly, by Angelo. 'That leaves me out of it. I was nowhere near the kitchen, and I wasn't seated at his table.'

His callous indifference to the fact that Richard may have been murdered only goes to confirm that the Memphis homicide rate is off the charts.

Larkin is not impressed. 'Let me be clear. This investigation is now in the hands of the Criminal Investigation Unit of the RCMP. No one is going anywhere until all of you have been thoroughly questioned. When the weather clears, a team of investigators will be arriving from RCMP Headquarters in St. John's to conduct the interviews. In the meantime, I expect detailed, signed witness statements from each of you. ASAP.'

That shuts up Angelo in short order.

Carmel Ann timidly raises her hand.

There's a sharp *yes*.

'May I, sir, address the matter of accommodation? We are due to check out of the inn by eleven tomorrow morning.'

'The manager has been contacted. There were only two reservations following yours. Because of the storm, one was rescheduled, the other cancelled. You are all to stay exactly where you are.'

'I see. Thank you.'

Just when they thought they had warmed up, a chill settled over the seating area, rendering the KNOT exec immobile. Outlier Angelo, now stiffly upright, squirms about, trying to look comfortable.

I raise my hand assuredly. 'As I have previously mentioned to our group, Staff Sergeant Larkin, Mae and I have had experience completing witness statements and would be more than willing to assist anyone who might require help.'

'Constables O'Rourke and Blanchett are entirely capable of doing that. Thank you.'

He's put me in my place without a moment's hesitation. I see.

I do have a countermeasure. Let's see if he'll remain quite so dismissive when I bring up the matter of the blue canister in Tryphena's overnight case.

I'll admit it will take a delicate approach, given the clandestine manner in which the canister was uncovered.

In the meantime, what's Larkin's next move? Has he arrived with a search warrant for the room of the person who had the most contact with the Martin meal?

The others begin to disperse, presumably to work on their witness statements. As they do, Larkin has an additional directive. 'If you need to go to your room to retrieve what you have composed so far, please do so promptly. I suggest finding a table in the dining room. One of the constables will accompany each of you to your room. When everyone is back and seated, they will assist you as needed.'

I have to talk to him ASAP, before Tryphena has the opportunity to get rid of the canister. Fortunately, it won't flush down her toilet.

When the last of the five has wandered off, I nod to Mae and we approach Larkin together.

'Staff Sergeant, this is urgent. There's something we need to make you aware of.'

He can't ignore my tone of voice. Not that he's expecting much. 'Yes.'

Here we go. 'Other than a tour guide, I have a second occupation. I'm a registered private detective.'

I pause to let that take hold. Larkin, however, shows no surprise.

'Your name surfaced when I spoke to Inspector Bowmore. She noticed it on the list I sent her, the list of those who had direct contact with Richard Martin at the time of the incident. She confirmed your secondary line of work.'

A rather listless delivery, Staff Sergeant Larkin. Old news, is it? I shouldn't be surprised, at either the indifference or the trail of RCMP information.

Inspector Bowmore, head of the Criminal Investigation Unit, and I go way back. Professionally and, as a matter of fact, personally. (Sorry, Larkin, I'm not about to go there.)

I would hope that my line of work is not all that the inspector confirmed. She's only too aware of my reputation from the several cases we've worked on together.

'The next time you're in contact, please pass along my regards.'

That amplifies the alliance I have with his superior. As I now see it, Officer, it's a very useful state of affairs.

'Earlier this morning, with the storm intensifying, we came to the conclusion that it was unlikely you would make it here with a search warrant. In my capacity as a private detective, and due to the fact that time was critical, I entered the vacant room of Tryphena Loveless, whom I assume is a prime suspect in this case, to investigate whether there might possibly be evidence of a link to what appeared to be the fatal allergic reaction of Richard Martin.'

'Stop right there.'

I thought I was doing a very good job of it. Well-worded, very logical.

'You had her permission to do this?'

'I can't say I did—'

'The door was open,' injects Mae.

Not open open, but open as in unlocked. Not something he needs to know.

'The term, Mr. Synard, is *break and enter*.'

'I didn't take anything.'

'In the eyes of the law—entirely irrelevant.'

Rather than have this go on ad nauseam, I take out my phone. I sprint into photos and turn the screen toward Larkin. 'In Tryphena's overnight case. Japanese. Shellfish seasoning powder.'

Mae's phone is next in line, with the screenshot of the translated list of ingredients from the back of the canister.

Larkin is speechless, if only for the time it takes him to dismount from his high horse. 'I have a search warrant. We'll see for ourselves.'

'If the canister is still there.'

"If" awaiting the execution of a search warrant.

Needless to say, the show of police force causes quite an uproar. Not only had Larkin come bearing one search warrant, he came with a grand total of six, one for each of the occupied rooms in the inn. And, as he is quick to point out, all have been formally authorized by the regional court judge.

The rooms belong to the five unsuspecting individuals assembled in the dining room, dutifully working on their witness statements, plus that of yours truly. I am the sole person not alarmed and pleading for (in Angelo's case, demanding) an explanation.

Larkin is more than up to the task. 'Let me remind you that the RCMP is treating this as possible first-degree murder. The Criminal Investigation Unit has advised me to conduct these searches because the arrival of the officers has been delayed by the storm. Your cooperation, under the Canadian Criminal Code, is mandatory. So sit back, return to what you were doing, complete your witness statements. I assure you we'll be respectful of your possessions, and they will be left in the same condition that we find them.'

'But, sir,' declares Bobbie, 'that's my private space.'

The urgency in her voice leads me to imagine just what might be uncovered in Bobbie's private space. And I'm not talking incriminating evidence. I glance, wide-eyed, at Mae.

'Again, I assure you we will exercise discretion in regard to your personal items, whatever they might be.' Larkin smiles to reassure her. Is that a knowing smile? Bobbie's room might be in for an especially thorough search.

Wisely, Bobbie says nothing more. If the others have any other points to make, they also wisely keep them to themselves.

My attention is, of course, directed to Tryphena in particular. Surprisingly, she doesn't appear especially agitated. Which leads me to believe that the blue canister is no longer in her room, that she removed it at some point prior to going into her room with the constable to collect the laptop that sits on the table in front of her.

A tote bag bearing the tag line *Read on! Right on!* hangs off the back of her chair. Could that be where the canister lies, despite the fact the tote is looking rather two-dimensional? Or did Tryphena somehow dispose of the canister?

It's the sole topic of the conversation I have with Mae, now that the three officers have gone off to execute the search warrants and those left in the room are glued to their chairs. At least for now, in anticipation of the officers' return. It's going to take a while.

Mae and I have quietly removed ourselves from the dining room to a corner of the empty corridor. The exchange is quick and to the point.

'If she did dispose of it, where?'

'No going outside to bury it. Not in this storm.'

'Besides, there was no time.'

'Someplace she could hide it and go back to. Then retrieve it and get rid of it permanently.'

'Close by, somewhere to slip in and out of quickly.'

'The kitchen,' we declare decisively.

Logical. No-nonsense. Door always open. Standing invite for a glass of water, juice. Cup of tea, coffee.

Within seconds we're in the kitchen. Two glasses of water on the counter in record time. Four hands opening cupboards, looking for hiding spots. The options are scant—soup tureen, partial bag of flour, tub of dishwasher pods.

Dual in-cabinet, pullout receptacles—one for recyclables, one for garbage headed for the landfill. Both roughly half full.

'Go for it.'

I pull back the sleeve of my sweatshirt and tentatively plunge my arm into the garbage bin. It's a disgusting mess. I hold my breath and fish around, through what I take to be the scrapings from breakfast, mixed with slimy plastic wrap, greasy paper towels, generalized kitchen crud. I'm fishing for something solid, the size of the canister.

And, by the hell, that something is there. Sunk almost to the bottom.

My limb surfaces, rancid. In my hand is the fugitive, crud-smeared canister. As Mae confirms, it's absolutely blue and branded in foreign script. She snaps a photo.

There is no point in retaining the canister. Better that Larkin uncovers it himself. I force it back into the offal depths and head for the kitchen sink while Mae trails behind me with a paper towel, wiping up what's dripping onto the floor.

I scour my hand and forearm with dish detergent and dry them vigorously with several more paper towels, all of which are deposited in the garbage bin, neatly covering any recent disturbance below.

Just as I shut the cabinet drawer, in walks the ever-unpredictable Angelo.

'Juice?' I enquire. 'Water, tap or sparkling?'

'Why aren't you completing your witness statement like the rest of us?'

'Almost done. All it needs is a little touch-up.' Not quite true. The fact is I had planned on working on it before breakfast this morning, and then Mae showed up. None of which is any of Angelo's business, regardless.

'You two seem to be doing a lot of moving about. Looks like the cops have put you to work.'

Confine your theorizing to toponymy, Mr. Jones. Otherwise you're making a fool of yourself (which I realize is not hard to do).

My verbal response avoids another flare-up. 'We like to keep hydrated.' I retrieve a glass from a cabinet and hand it to him. 'I suggest you do the same.'

When he makes no move to take it, I set it on the counter and exit the kitchen, Mae close behind.

The guy makes me want to vent. 'Dickhead,' I mutter as we head toward the seating area.

'Why is he keeping an eye on us? What's it to him?'

'You're thinking it's something more than being a natural pain in the ass?'

'I'm thinking we should dig into his background,' Mae says. 'See if it triggers anything.'

We don't have many tools at our disposal. The guy lives half a continent away.

'What do you know about AI background checks?' Mae asks.

'You're talking the States. Potential legal issues. Wouldn't touch it with a ten-foot pole. Besides, there's no time. And it costs.'

We keep it old school—websites, Facebook. With the hope of finding something recent that sparks our interest.

So there we sit with our phones, in sight of the person whose name we're sending through the search engines. I'm tempted to make eye contact and smugly smile. Probably not a good idea.

The name *Angelo Jones* (in this case, appropriately enough) is as common as dog shit. There's at least 106 of them living in Memphis. Adding *toponymy* to the search terms does help.

He has a website with profile, books and articles authored, etc.— nothing more than what was in the conference brochure. The news section of the website was last updated two years ago.

'Got him,' Mae whispers. She's been focusing on Facebook.

As it turns out, what she's got is much the same stuff, reconfigured to make him look more personable. The picture with his wife suggests he hasn't succeeded. And the one with their German shepherd, named Wolf, leads me to think the mutt could potentially take a piece out of his hide without thinking twice.

As for the other photos—mostly images of road signs from places he's made a point of visiting—there's nothing to write home about. (Other than *Fugging*, in Austria, which, to his disappointment, had changed its name from *Fucking* a month before his long trek to get there. A costly miscalculation on his part.)

Mae and I have come up empty-handed. At the moment, Angelo is staring our way, as if attempting to uproot us from whatever it is we've been fixated on. He figures we're up to no good.

Quite the opposite, Angelo Jones. What we're up to at the moment is pairing your name with *Japan* to see if Google's AI Overviews come up with anything whatsoever that might link you to the canister that has turned out to be Exhibit A—swimming, for the moment only, among the dregs of kitchen garbage.

I am constantly amazed at what AI can uncover in no time flat. "There are several notable Angelo Joneses associated with Japan," it tells me authoritatively. That includes a translator who works at Mitsubishi; the head of Beyond Sushi, a tour company specializing in culinary tours of Kyoto; and a photographer whose shots of Japan's avant-garde street-fashion scene are huge on TikTok.

Who knew? Not that it's any help whatsoever.

'Go to Images,' whispers Mae excitedly. 'Scroll down.'

I do my best to ignore the outrageously dressed females strutting around Tokyo. 'What am I looking for?'

'A line of five men, all in suits, looking overly serious, standing in front of a map of East Asia.' They leap off the screen in contrast to the Tokyo fashionistas.

OMG. That's him. Which is doubly off-putting because when I look up, there's himself in the flesh staring at me.

We do our best to appear nonchalant. The Angelo Jones in the photo is on the far right, taller and rotund compared to the other four, looking especially uncool. (Although I admit he has little competition.)

The link from the photo reveals that all five were speakers at a forum on East Asian toponymy that took place in Osaka three months earlier.

So the man went to Japan recently, undoubtedly after he accepted the invitation to Gutted: Fervent Focus on Newfoundland Toponymy. When he flew out of Osaka, did he happen to have in his luggage the same blue canister (a.k.a. Exhibit A) that's lingering in the kitchen trash, waiting to be uncovered by a staff sergeant of the Royal Canadian Mounted Police?

If I were you, Angelo Jones, I'd wipe the arrogant expression off that mug of yours.

I take a screen shot of the Osaka Five, and after a few seconds of scrolling through the street-fashion crowd, return my phone to a pocket. Mae does the same with hers.

We bide our time. We feign intimate conversation, calculated to drive the acclaimed toponymist nuts. I figured I'm owed a little self-satisfaction.

When all is said and done, the trio of officers finally reappears. They stand dauntlessly before us all, presumably prepared to give an account of their forays into the guest rooms.

I gently intercede. I raise my hand to Larkin, then direct it to one side as I get to my feet, in a single coordinated gesture that tells him we need to talk, in private. I lead him past the open door to the kitchen. The constables follow. As does Mae. Yes, something is definitely up. I close the door behind us.

'What's with you?' Larkin says.

His irritation I quickly set aside. He's found no blue canister in Tryphena's room, or any evidence of one. I pull out the cabinet and direct his attention to the very place it can be found if he'd just take a moment to dig in and get to the bottom of this mess.

'You want me to sink my arm into that on the speculation that the canister is down there somewhere?'

'I'd aim for the bottom if I were you.'

Mae calls up the photo on her phone and sweeps it before all three officers. 'It's for real, I'm afraid.'

Larkin is still hesitant. An officer of his rank is not about to roll up the sleeve of his pristine shirt and take the plunge. He has a constable for just such an eventuality.

Constable Blanchett takes the hint. 'I don't mind, sir.'

He does mind, of course. It's a nasty business, as I well know. A nasty business that goes on much longer than it should.

'I'm certain there's nothing here fitting that description, sir,' says Blanchett as he continues to swirl his hands deep in the slime.

'Enough,' declares Larkin. 'Withdraw and wash up.' He turns to me, disgusted. 'A huge waste of time, Mr. Synard. Just what's up with you?'

I struggle for words.

Mae not so. 'Angelo Jones stole it.'

I hadn't thought of that. But of course she's right!

'He came into the kitchen as we were leaving,' adds Mae. 'He knew it was there and suspected we also knew.'

I finish her thoughts. 'So he dug out the canister and made off with it, the bugger. Where it is now is anybody's guess. But one thing for sure—Angelo Jones is in cahoots with Tryphena Loveless.'

It's all too much for the three Mounties to get their heads around, especially when I present them with the picture of the Osaka toponymists.

Mae thinks a summary would help. 'Angelo Jones confirmed he would be speaking at the conference in Newfoundland and knew that Richard Martin would also be there.

'At the same time, Jones, having learned from one of the organizers, Tryphena Loveless, that Richard Martin has a severe allergy to shellfish, purchases a canister of shellfish seasoning, either on his own initiative or at the request of Ms. Loveless. This is so that the two, working together, can poison Mr. Martin at the time they all come together for Gutted: Fervent Focus on Newfoundland Toponymy.'

Nicely put, Mae. And to my mind, convincing.

'And the motive? What do you see as the reason they would want him dead?'

Larkin's question is directed at Mae, but I don't hesitate to fill in the blank. 'It became quite clear during the conference that Angelo Jones had an intense dislike for Richard Martin. I would say, with further investigation, the reason why it escalated to murder will fall into place.'

'And Ms. Loveless, what's the motive?'

'Again, I'm certain it will become clear in time.'

'You hope.'

Rather snarky, but I let it pass. 'The fact is, a canister of what is essentially poison was found in the woman's luggage.' That reality is staring Larkin in the face. It's about time he made a move to deal with it.

'I'll be frank, Mr. Synard. We need the bloody canister. Without it, there's no proof of anything.'

Larkin's got to be kidding. 'We have the photograph. How could she deny it was there, in her suitcase?'

'She could say she knows nothing about it. She could say someone planted it. A someone who wanted to shift the blame to her.'

'Like who?'

'Like you. For example.'

For example? How good of him to add that! Jesus.

'When it comes to a conviction,' Larkin says, 'surely your experience as a private detective has taught you the importance of concrete evidence versus someone's word. Especially if that word is coming from an individual who could also be considered a suspect.'

'Mae can confirm that I showed her the picture not five minutes after I took it!'

'No need to raise your voice, Mr. Synard.'

I suck in more air. 'She was also right here, standing next to me when I fished the can out of the garbage.'

'She's your partner, Mr. Synard. Any lawyer would argue she's far from an impartial witness.'

Jesus.

Calm down, Synard. You're making it worse on yourself. Larkin is in control, and there's sweet fuck all you can do about it. 'What the hell . . . I mean, what exactly do you intend to do at this point, Officer?'

Larkin opens the door and walks out of the kitchen, the two constables trailing behind him, leaving Mae and me standing there. She grips my arm and presses herself gently against me.

We have no choice but to follow them. We head back to the sofa, but Larkin abruptly intervenes and directs us to a vacant table. We sit, surrounded by the other five, who are scrutinizing us for clues as to what went on in the kitchen.

'Sorry for the delay,' Larkin tells them. 'In the meantime, as I look out the windows, I see the storm is starting to abate. A relief to everyone I'm sure.'

It's not the relief they're desperate for.

'We have completed a search of your rooms. Everything has been left as we found it.'

I glance at Tryphena. She's stonefaced. Then at smug, two-faced Angelo. The only one showing anything that vaguely resembles relief is Bobbie. I wonder why.

'The investigation, however, continues,' Larkin says. 'We await the arrival of the Criminal Investigation Unit from St. John's, which I expect will be mid-morning tomorrow.'

'Are we entitled to know the results of the search warrants?' It's Angelo, straining to look civil.

'At this point, you are not. I will be forwarding the results to the investigative team shortly. You will be made aware of them in the course of the interviews tomorrow. In the meantime,

I will collect your witness statements, copies of which will also be forwarded to the investigators. Constable O'Rourke will remain at the inn for the remainder of today and overnight. If you have questions, you are to direct them to her. She, of course, will be in direct contact with me should any clarification be needed.'

In other words, we've been placed on ice, awaiting further police action, while under guard. For me, at least, not surprising.

Not that I can conceive of anyone attempting to escape. What it does is cement the fact that the RCMP is firmly in control of the whereabouts of each one of us until such time as a decision is made about who might be released and who might be further detained.

Carmel Ann raises a hand hesitantly. 'What about food? We need to eat.'

Constable O'Rourke steps forward. 'I have been in touch with Pitcher's in New Harbour. Which, by the way, I can personally vouch for, having eaten there on several occasions. They are reopening as soon as the roads are plowed. In which case, we'll call in an order for takeout and I'll arrange delivery.'

'Thank you.' Carmel Ann sinks back meekly into her chair.

Her reaction is indicative of the pallor that has settled over the inn. It's been a long day, and it looks like it could be an even longer evening. Let's hope Pitcher's lives up to its reputation.

In the meantime, there's the ongoing saga of the witness statements. Since we don't have access to a printer, they are to be emailed to the RCMP detachment under the direction of one of the constables. The statements have to be dated and signed electronically, which for two of the exec begins with tedious, step-by-step instructions on how to go about downloading a program that will do just that.

Mort, in particular, is not a happy camper, but finally the individual statements are all signed, sealed, and delivered, ready to be printed when Larkin and Blanchett return to Harbour Grace.

Suddenly, all attention veers to the picture windows of the dining room. A hulk of a Department of Highways snowplow is muscling its way along the road in front of the inn. Still not the relief the KNOT crew is desperate for.

As for Larkin, although he's not desperate, it is a relief, and the impetus he's been waiting for. 'We'll clue-up and head back,' he announces.

Right away? As if there's not an outstanding issue that requires his attention.

Isn't he going to question Angelo or Tryphena? Is he really about to bugger off, presumably because—mastermind that he is—he's concluded it's something that can wait until morning, when the St. John's brain trust finally gets here?

Larkin has given no merit whatsoever to anything Mae and I have told him about the goddamn blue canister.

Mae can see I'm pissed. I make a move to deal with him. She lays a hand on my shoulder and applies enough pressure that I sit back down.

'His mind is made up,' she says. 'You don't want to rattle his cage any more than you already have.'

She's right, I guess. Pathetic though the situation is.

Larkin does have a few words for me after taking to his taxpayer-funded parka, gloves, muskrat hat, and Ford F-250. A few words in private and of his own initiative no less.

'First, to put it bluntly, where the hell is your witness statement? It's not among the others.'

'I ran out of time.'

'Not good enough, Synard. Get it to me pronto.'

I look agreeable.

'Second, when I get back to the detachment, I'll be doing some background checks. If anything shows up, I'll text you.' He requests my number.

It's something. Far from enough, but something.

Mae is surprised he would even do that much.

'Inspector Bowmore,' I remind her. 'When he was talking to Bowmore, she bloody well told him I deserve some respect.'

'Very good.' Trying to keep it upbeat.

'Just not enough respect that he was willing to deal with the business of the goddamn canister.'

The cage rattling continues. Larkin's gone and I'm left sorry he's oblivious to it.

SEVEN: LUSHES BIGHT

THE DINING ROOM has emptied. We assume everyone is back in their respective rooms, coming to terms with the notion that the RCMP just rifled through their personal belongings. Constable O'Rourke is nowhere to be seen.

Mae and I decide to decompress by standing in front of the picture windows and breathing in the wider, snow-covered, poststorm world before sitting snugly together on one of the sofas. Through it all, we have each other. That's the positive.

It is not long before the negative resurrects itself.

'God only knows what Angelo did with the canister,' Mae says.

'We could confront him.' Then, on second thought, 'Probably not such a great idea.'

'He'd deny everything. It would just get nasty, and we'd be no further ahead.'

'What about Tryphena? She knows we know something is up. If she only suspected it before, Dickhead sure as heck confirmed it. How about we lay our cards on the table and see how she reacts?'

'Also probably not such a good idea,' says Mae. 'She's not going to admit to anything. Word will get back to Angelo, and there'll be more shit to deal with. I think it's better to wait until the investigators get here. We'll at least have an inn thick with cops if things get out of hand.'

Multiple Mounties as opposed to lone Constable O'Rourke, who now reappears, looking a little done in by the world outside. The fur on her muskrat hat is tipped with snow, even if the rest of her has been brushed clean.

'Not much falling now,' she tells us. Which doesn't explain why she was outside for so long, well beyond the time we saw the Ford F-250 make it out of the driveway and onto the plowed road.

Whether we're due an explanation, she's yet to decide. She deposits her winter gear in the closet and takes a seat on the opposite sofa. A pleasant enough smile, but no words to accompany it.

Her phone dings. A quick read and she puts it away.

'The staff sergeant wants you to know that I didn't find anything.'

Our puzzled looks will hopefully serve as a prompt.

'The canister. I dug around outside. No luck.'

Which begs my question. 'The staff sergeant thought it might have been tossed out into the snow?'

'I did. It was my suggestion. He gave me the go-ahead. I was looking for indentations.'

'Really?'

'There were none. If there was a canister and it did get flung outside, then it was buried by the drifting snow.'

Makes some sense. I have to give her points for initiative.

'I focused on the area outside the side door.'

A bit of a slog to get through all that snow. But a logical tactic. Not that logic turned out to be in any way productive.

'We'll just have to wait until the snow melts,' Mae says. A way of bringing the exchange to a conclusion. We don't want to be dwelling on an odd miscalculation.

I will say this in Constable O'Rourke's favour. Unlike Larkin she appears to have faith that there is a blue canister somewhere and it is indeed an important element in the investigation.

In other words, she's an ally. She's on our side of the investigative fence.

'So, Constable, where do you suggest we go from here?'

She's not liking the sound of that. 'What do you mean?'

'I mean what else can we try to advance the investigation?'

She's liking the sound of that even less. 'My assignment is to maintain a secure perimeter, to make sure no one leaves.'

'But undoubtedly, if there is suspicious activity, you would record it and report it to the staff sergeant.'

'I'm not sure where this is leading, Mr. Synard.'

I'll take the plunge and hope she buys into it. 'In my experience, Constable, I often find it necessary to set up a scenario with a suspect in order to analyze his or her response, with the expectation that it will reveal something crucial to the case.'

Impressive as that might sound, it hasn't upped her comfort level. I press on.

'For example, let's say at supper you make a point of sitting with Tryphena. You chit-chat for a while, and then you inquire as to how she became interested in catering. As she eases into the conversation you then ask, are there some food cultures you like in particular?'

Mae quickly surmised where I'm going with this. She jumps in, 'Then at some point, you casually remark, "Have you tried cooking Japanese?" If she says *yes*, you ask, "Where do you get your ingredients?" If she says *no*, then you say, "I imagine ingredients are hard to get, especially things like seasonings."'

Remarkable, Mae. It's back to me. 'All the while, of course, you're observing any change in her behaviour. Is she getting agitated? Is she quick to change the conversation? Especially when you say the word "seasonings."'

Constable O'Rourke is struggling for a response. She's on the brink, and it's not looking good.

'If I could be so bold,' I add quickly, 'it would be a very practical use of your suppertime.'

'Then why don't you do it?' she blurts out. 'You two sit with her. You ask the questions.'

'For the simple reason it would backfire. Ms. Loveless is deadly suspicious of us. In her mind, she's our prime suspect.'

'Besides,' says Mae. 'We'll be sitting with Angelo.'

We will? 'Yes, we will.'

'Doing what you would be doing with Tryphena,' Mae adds. 'Asking questions, discreetly probing.'

'Teamwork,' I assert. 'Working together to advance the investigation.'

Then, just when it's do or die with the constable, Carmel Ann shows up.

Her arrival does nothing to alleviate the tension. In fact it adds to it. She's tightly wound.

'Your supper orders—I need them now. Pitcher's menu is online.'

'It's only four-thirty,' says Mort.

'That's too bad,' says Carmel Ann. Today's events have done her in.

'Give me your cell numbers. I'll send you the link. We need to get this over and done with.'

'Yes, ma'am.' Followed by a quick salute.

She comes close to snarling at me. I dutifully scan the menu and make my choices.

'For drinks—a half-dozen beer,' she says. 'I have no clue . . . '

'I like IPA,' I tell her.

'Whatever comes comes.'

It's her way or the highway. Speaking of which . . .

'I've been in contact with Constable Blanchett,' O'Rourke tells Carmel Ann. 'The roads are all passable, at reduced speeds. Safe enough for take-out delivery. You're good to call anytime. Ask Pitcher's to have it ready by six.'

Who O'Rourke has in mind for pickup and delivery is anybody's guess. The Sprinter is off the list. The vehicles belonging to Carmel Ann and Mae are both snowed in and going nowhere, and there's been no mention of a taxi company because, I suspect, Dildo is too small to have one.

Constable O'Rourke is now on her phone, scanning her contacts.

'PJ, it's O'Rourke here. I need a favour.'

I have the answer to my question. At 6:10 p.m. Constable O'Rourke and I have walked the tracks left by the Ford F-250 and are at the end of the driveway, collecting the two boxes of food and beer just delivered in a pickup.

'Thanks, PJ. You're a godsend.'

'No sweat.' The woman smiles and pumps her fist. 'Can't wait, can you?' Then chants, '"We don't play with Barbie dolls . . ."'

O'Rourke jumps in, '"We just play with bats and balls."'

PJ reverses the pickup and is gone. The constable leads the way back to the inn. I follow, clueless.

'Slow-pitch softball,' the constable calls back to me. 'We're on the same team. Last season PJ was the league's MVP.'

Initially dumbfounded, I'm now in the game. It puts me in the mood for an IPA.

As it turns out, Dildo's Glorious and Free IPA, 6.5% ABV. I retrieve it from the box before anyone else lays eyes on it and sit back on the sofa, where Mae and I will wait until we see which table Angelo chooses.

My phone vibrates. I check the caller ID. It's Heather Simpson. I was wondering why she hasn't been in touch. I keep my voice low and out of the hearing range of the others gathering for supper.

'Of course I didn't make it out to Harbour Grace due to the weather,' Heather tells me. 'I emailed my witness statement to the detachment. Larkin hasn't been in touch.'

'He's been up to his neck, and it's not just the snow.' I fill her in on what the RCMP and the Dildo inn crowd have all been up to since last evening.

'Wow.' It takes her a moment to absorb it all. 'Sounds like an ordeal.'

'The canister business keeps us going. It's the linchpin.'

'Is there room for a second linchpin?'

A jolt to the neurons.

'I would have been in touch earlier, but I wanted to double-check I got it right.'

Like an investigative reporter would. My breath is on hold.

'Tryphena Loveless . . . Until two years, ago Tryphena Loveless was married to Richard Martin.'

My jaw hits the floor. 'You're kidding.'

'Like you, I had this feeling that there was far more to Tryphena Loveless than meets the eye. I did a little poking around. She was Triffie Martin, but changed back to her birth name.'

I won't ask where she got all this. Reporters have their sources.

'From what I've been told, the divorce was nasty. She accused her husband of having an affair with a much younger woman, which he denied. In the end, they settled out of court. I don't know the terms, but she left St. John's and went back to the family home in Fair Haven, which had been left vacant after her parents died.'

I'm marvelling. Stunned but marvelling.

'Are you still there?'

Recovered, I state the obvious. 'What do you think? Was the divorce so nasty that she was out for revenge?'

'For me it's an open question. What do *you* think?'

I'm not sure what to think, except . . . 'It needs further investigation. At my end, not yours.'

'Resentment has a way of festering,' she says.

'Then resurfacing.'

'Good luck.'

That I'll need. We disconnect, I fill in an anxious Mae, and the two of us head straight for Constable O'Rourke. Thankfully, she's yet to sit down. Nor has Tryphena made an appearance in the dining room.

I convince the constable to accompany us into the empty hallway. I hurriedly fill her in on the conversation with Heather.

'How does she know all this?' Meaning, are her sources to be trusted.

It's not the time for skepticism. 'I have no reason not to believe her.'

The urgency in my voice does little to convince the officer. 'I have to think about it,' O'Rourke says.

In other words, she needs time to run it by her boss.

But there is no time. The door to Tryphena's room opens and out she comes. Unsmiling, she walks past us and into the dining room. I step closer to its entrance. Sure enough she's heading to a vacant table.

'It's now or never, Constable.'

That's it. That's the extent of the pressure I can apply to the police officer without hopelessly pissing her off.

Not only that, but a second glance inside the dining room tells me Angelo is also about to sit down, also by himself. Mae and I turn off our phones in preparation for an uninterrupted exchange.

We arrive at Angelo's table just as he takes his seat.

'I'm sure you wouldn't mind if we join you,' says the dauntless Mae. 'We thought we should reach out in an attempt to be on friendlier terms.'

Bullshit, of course. What we're about to attempt is to get him talking, enough that something might inadvertently slip out, adding another piece—no matter how small—to the puzzle.

'In fact, I do mind.'

He stands up and pushes in his chair, then stalks off to an empty table as far away from us as he can get.

We're left stuck to our chairs, silenced. I crack open my IPA and down a defiant mouthful.

'Oh, well,' says Mae. She speaks for both of us.

In the meantime, Carmel Ann is calling out the various orders, handing the boxes—one at a time—to Constable O'Rourke, who delivers them to the tables.

'For drinks,' announces the KNOT president, 'there's ice water and Dildo beer. Your choice. If it's IPA you're looking for, you're out of luck. If you want tea or coffee, the kitchen is there, you're on your own. *Bon appétit.*'

End of obligations. Carmel Ann clutches the last box, grabs a beer, spies our table, then sits down in the renegade's vacant seat, uninvited.

'I saw him give you the finger, so to speak. I figured you need a little moral support.'

Carmel Ann makes for a challenging consolation prize. Her fiery mood continues. She's in no frame of mind to pussyfoot around the question that's on everyone's mind. Except the mind of at least one person, whoever that person is.

Our meal boxes remain unopened. 'Who do you think did it, Sebastian?' When I don't answer right away, she adds, 'I've excluded you for two reasons. One, you're here by chance, not because you made a point of being here. Two, I look at you and ask myself what could you possibly gain by poisoning Richard? Nothing.'

'That's good to know.' Again, the humour is lost on her.

So in Carmel Ann's eyes, I'm a suspect in name only. Can I say the same for her? Have I scratched her off my list of suspects, or accomplices for that matter?

'I know what you're thinking,' she says. 'Is there any chance it could have been me? No. Otherwise why would I be raising the topic? To focus attention on myself? Obviously not.'

She has a point. In any case, I have a gut feeling she isn't the murdering type. I'll go with my gut, at least for now.

'We're down to four possibilities,' I say. 'If we eliminate the catering staff.'

'Which I think we can because, like you, they didn't plan to be there at the time. They're hired help.'

'They did have ready access to the kitchen. Someone could have paid one of them to contaminate Richard's meal.'

'A hired killer recruited in Winterton? Doesn't jibe with me.'

'Me neither.'

'Okay, so we're down to four. Who had it in for Richard and why?'

Like I said, no pussyfooting. But no way am I about to mention the canister to her, or even the divorce. That's exclusively material for the cops and the certified PI. That is, one of the hired help who happened to show up to the scene of the crime.

'Like you, Carmel Ann,' says Mae, 'we both can speculate, but any finger pointing is best left to the RCMP.'

Thanks, Mae. Carmel Ann can do with an outsider perspective.

'So that's why the constable is having a little heart-to-heart with Triffie.' Carmel Ann is staring behind Mae and I.

Nonchalantly, we turn, one at a time, to the table where, indeed, Constable O'Rourke is in conversation with

Tryphena Loveless (formerly Martin). The subject in question has her back to us.

I take a moment to privately applaud the constable for stepping up to the plate in the way she did. The game looks to be going well. No sign of striking out.

'Interesting,' I say to Carmel Ann.

'Very.'

'There seems to be more to Triffie than meets the eye,' says Mae.

'Really? Why would you say that?'

'I take her to be used to what a city has to offer. I'm wondering what she finds in Fair Haven to occupy her time. It has so few people, and it's far off the beaten track.'

'She does travel. And she loves to read,' says Carmel Ann. As if that's enough to end the conversation. 'Our meals are getting cold.'

I open the box in front of me. The two-piece fish and chips looks up, disappointed I didn't get to it earlier.

Mae fares better with her clubhouse sandwich. And as for Carmel Ann, what the online menu described as meat-lover's pizza looks to be exactly that. Pepperoni, salami, bacon, sausage, ground beef . . . It has it all. The cheese and tomato sauce are hardly existent.

I hate to admit it, but I'm hit with meal regret. It's happened before. I'm in a restaurant, the meals arrive, and suddenly I'm wishing I had ordered what's on the plate next to me. I glance into the open box in front of Carmel Ann and practically salivate. I'll never learn.

As Carmel Ann works her way through the pizza and sips her Stout Dildo purposefully, she seems to quickly lose her appetite.

'Let's not beat around the bush,' she says. 'Triffie is at the top of the list, just because she spent so much time in the kitchen. What about Mort? The man did go in the kitchen at one point.'

'In that case, what about Bobbie?' I'm playing the devil's advocate. 'Who's to say she didn't wander into the kitchen?'

'Bobbie was with me the whole time,' says Carmel Ann. 'Before and after we sat down. She wasn't out of my sight.'

'And Angelo?' says Mae.

'How do you propose he got into the kitchen and out again without being noticed?' says Carmel Ann.

'He could be an accomplice,' I point out.

The idea hadn't entered her mind. She takes several moments to respond. 'You mean Angelo came up with the plan, and someone else carried it out?'

'I'm not saying he did. I'm saying it's possible.'

'That means . . . ' Carmel Ann is not about to go there.

Mae does it for her. 'That means anyone on the list of suspects could be an accomplice. He or she needn't be the person who actually contaminated the meal.'

'You mean . . . '

'In the eyes of the RCMP, not having personal access to Richard's meal doesn't eliminate you or anyone else from the list of suspects.'

Now I see where Mae is going with this. Her aim is to throw uncertainty into Carmel Ann's fixation on Tryphena, to ensure she doesn't confront her.

'Even me,' I say, to boost the impact. 'I could have plotted with you, for example, and supplied you with the poison, and then you had Tryphena put the finishing touch to the meal in the kitchen.'

Now Carmel Ann is thoroughly confounded.

Mae turns her attention to the clubhouse sandwich in the open box in front of her. I look down at my fish and chips and fake satisfaction before I begin plowing my way through them.

Carmel Ann closes the cover on what's left of her pizza. She works at finding some consolation in what's left of the Stout Dildo, but even that leaves her looking drained.

'As good as mine is, I think I've had my fill,' announces Mae. 'Anyone interested in half a clubhouse?'

Certainly not Carmel Ann. In which case I shut the lid on the fish and chips and take Mae up on her offer.

'What we all need is a good night's sleep,' I tell the sullen president between bites.

'Fat chance.'

That about sums her up. Carmel Ann is desperate for an end to all this turmoil but is freaked out at the thought of how much more she'll have to endure.

'The investigative squad should provide some clarity,' I tell her, trying to sound more optimistic than I actually am.

'Don't get your hopes up.' And with that, Carmel Ann pushes back her chair. Grabbing the box, she heads out of the dining room by way of a waste bin. There, she dumps both the box and the can, not bothering to separate the latter into the recycling bin next to it.

'Well,' says Mae. 'That was food for thought.' She's not smiling.

I take the last bite of the clubhouse and the last trickle of IPA.

'You think there's more to Carmel Ann than meets the eye?' she asks.

'She just wants this situation over and done with.'

Mae shrugs. 'As we all do.'

'She's president of KNOT. She's feeling extra responsibility for having invited Richard.'

'There's more to it than that.'

'You're detecting something that I'm not?'

'Possibly.'

I wait longer than I expect to. She's unsure. In which case it's only going to add another twist to an already twisted investigation.

'Do you think there's a possibility that Carmel Ann and Bobbie are a twosome?' Mae says. 'They seem to spend a lot of time together.'

See what I mean? Out of the blue and never crossed my mind. 'As in lovers? They do have separate rooms. What possible reason would they have to hide it?'

'Not lovers. Potentially, perhaps. But for now keeping close company, testing the waters.'

Which, to my mind, is superfluous. 'So what if they are? What difference would it make?'

'I get the impression the conference was their joint idea, in which case they have been connecting for months. What if they had a mutual dislike for what Richard stood for? What if they then discovered a mutual dislike for him as a person?'

'Enough that they would want him dead?' I ask Mae 'That's stretching it.'

'Add Tryphena to the picture, and that adds a new impetus. And remember, the intention may well have been just to prevent him speaking, not to do him in.'

Okay. A few breaths to give me time to get in stride.

'I'll take it as a possibility.' Not that we need another one. Just when I was heading with reasonable confidence in one direction, there's a fork in the road.

'And there's another possibility,' Mae says.

A third fork. 'Okay, lay it on me. I'm all ears.'

'Carmel Ann and Bobbie could have acted on their own, but once Richard died, a panic set in, at which point they planted that canister in Tryphena's luggage.'

'Planted the canister. Really? How would they have gotten into her room without her knowledge?' I ask.

'You managed it without much problem.'

Point taken. Let's move on. 'What about Angelo? Where is he in all this?'

'The more I think about it, the more I have to admit that's up for debate. If Angelo did purchase the canister and Tryphena was involved—either alone or with Carmel Ann and Bobbie—then Angelo would have agreed to it before he went to Japan, which was three months ago,' Mae says. 'But, according to Carmel Ann, Tryphena was not involved in KNOT until the planning of the conference was well under way, which was likely after he had been in Japan.'

I'm relieved she has doubts. I wouldn't want the theory to be bulletproof.

'In which case the canister could have been mail-ordered.'

Where there's a will, there's a way. 'And what about Mort?' In jest, of course. 'I would hate to see him left out, now that you have three of the four in on the action.'

'And then there's you, technically also a suspect, whom—at this point at least—I've excluded.' Mae adds a nod and a wink. 'Then again, you do have this thing about place names.'

Such a sweetheart. I may just have to prove my manly self more worthy of her respect. I offer a sultry smile.

We'll save that thought for later.

The priority is a head-to-head with Constable O'Rourke. She has just parted company with Tryphena, who makes her exit, presumably back to her room.

Angelo is the next to retreat. Of the others, only Bobbie and Mort are left. Interestingly enough, they have come together at one table and are now deep in conversation, oblivious to anyone one else in the dining room.

The constable is more than willing to talk to us. She looks eager, in fact, to get it over with. It's back to the sofas for what would appear to Bobbie and Mort, should they look our way, as a casual conversation. In any case, they are out of hearing range.

Constable O'Rourke's eagerness takes hold. 'Tryphena's never been to Japan and has no intention of ever going. And as for any indication of her present marital situation, she did say, and I quote, "I go through life never expecting it to be a bowl of cherries. Period."'

Surely, a conversation of fifteen or twenty minutes produced something more substantial than trite metaphor. 'What else did you talk about, if you don't mind me asking?'

'The weather, obviously. Softball. She was very interested to know what I did in my spare time.'

'What about what she did in *her* spare time?'

'She's a recluse from what I could tell. She likes to read.'

'That's it?' I say.

'She had no intention of going beyond that.'

'And you didn't push her?'

The constable has lost patience with me. 'Mr. Synard, I undertook your request against my better judgement. It's time you left the investigation in the hands of our Criminal Investigation Unit, which, as you are fully aware, will be arriving in the morning. In the meantime, I suggest you get a good night's sleep. And might I remind you, we have yet to receive your witness statement.'

It could be seen as putting me in my place. I prefer to think of it as the indication of an inexperienced young constable having reached the limits of her capabilities. In other words, she buggered up a prime opportunity and left us no further ahead in seeing what's behind the mask of Tryphena Loveless.

Enough said. Period.

All's quiet on the investigative front.

Although it's still light outside, everyone has retreated to their respective sleeping quarters, leaving Constable O'Rourke on the sofa, on guard duty. I suspect she'll eventually give in to the peace and quiet and stretch out for the night, a hand resting reassuringly on the holster of her Smith & Wesson.

I had considered asking her permission to walk down to the parking lot of the Dildo brewery, with a shovel to dig out the Sprinter. But in the end, I decide to wait until morning, when the parking lot of the inn is sure to be cleared.

This gives Mae and me a period of restless downtime. Restless because we're left with multiple scenarios as to how and why the poisoning of Richard Martin came about, without any further course of action that might offer new clues.

'Did you see how intently Mort and Bobbie were talking? What's up with that?'

Another theory. 'Let's not go there, Mae. Our plates are overflowing as it is.'

'So we do nothing pending the arrival of the RCMP squad?'

Although it may have come off sounding that way, I'm sure my nearest and dearest had no intention of characterizing us as gridlocked.

'Obviously, whoever is guilty no longer has any intention of talking to us,' I tell her. 'But let's face it, they're not going anywhere, and they have several hours ahead of them to ruminate on how exactly they'll respond to what the cops throw their way. The guilty are shit baked while the guiltless will be lying in bed half the night, fixated on who killed Richard and why. By morning, over breakfast, before the cops arrive, you're going to see accusations flare and red flags flying. Whoever did the deed or helped in any way will be squirming around the truth, doing whatever the hell they can to keep it from coming out.'

If that's gridlocked, then I might as well pack it in and tear up my PI certification.

'Point taken, Mr. Synard.' Mae's smirking. 'In which case I think I'll head to the shower. I think we should do what we can to chill out.'

'Sounds good to me.'

"Chill out" being a euphemism for any number of things. I'm game for chilling out.

While Mae's in the shower, I check my phone. Two missed calls. One from Nick, another from Frederick.

Nick is anxious for an update. It takes a while. It's been an eventful twenty-four hours.

'This is insane. Dad, man, what have you gotten yourself into?'

Good question. One I have no accurate answer for at the moment. 'We'll see.'

'I hope you and Mae are being careful.'

'We're under the very watchful eye of an officer of the RCMP. Tomorrow, the place will be maggoty with them.'

'In that case, stay on their good side.' A reminder of the fact that I have not always been in that position.

'How's Gaffer?' To change the subject.

'Good. Missing you, of course.'

Nothing like a dog to remind me there's a normal, uncomplicated life that, eventually, I'll return to. I can't wait.

'Love you both.'

'Love ya, Dad.' Gaffer gives an uplifting yelp in the background.

The call to Frederick Olsen is less affectionate.

'I didn't really have much to go on,' he says.

In other words, he struck out.

'Nothing in the court records, at least in what I have access to.'

'Divorce proceedings, possibly?'

'That requires a written formal request,' he says, 'and I would have to give justification. Helping out a private detective wouldn't qualify.'

I refrain from noting that, in the matter of divorce proceedings, he's been outsmarted by an investigative journalist.

'You might have more luck with Inspector Bowmore. She'll be out your way tomorrow.'

He and Bowmore have worked together in the past. Yet it's a surprise that the RCMP are talking it over with the RNC so early in the game. It must be that she's anticipating they could need Olsen's help. Why that would be, I don't quite get. I don't ask. I know Olsen would never tell me.

'I've been thinking Ailsa . . . Inspector Bowmore would show up,' I tell him, a reminder that, at times, we're on a first-name basis. 'If you want, I can keep you posted from my end. That way, you'll have two perspectives.'

A touch acerbic, just to keep the mutual respect in balance.

Olsen and I have what you might call a curious relationship. Going back years to when he abruptly stepped into the void left after Samantha and I divorced, back to when—because of the custody arrangement—he ended up spending more time with my son than I did. That got straightened out after a resentful few years, to the point Olsen and I learned to tolerate each other, and yes, on occasion, even appreciate each other's company over a dram or two of quality Scotch. That said, there remains a certain, shall we say, restraint between us, complicated by the fact that as a cop and a PI, we've found ourselves, on several occasions, on two sides of the same criminal activity.

You'd think we'd be able to separate the professional from the personal. Somehow, that's never quite the case. Mae will at times play the go-between, in an effort to normalize the relationship between the two couples, with reasonable success. Reasonable, but not yet wholehearted.

If it all sounds like I'm holding a grudge and it's about time I got over it, then all I can say is I am who I am, for better or worse.

'Time to say good night.'

'And good luck,' Olsen says.

'I'm all for that.'

As I said, a curious relationship.

I pour myself a much deserved dram of Glenmorangie. It's hard to relax. And then there's the matter of the witness statement.

Mae exits the washroom in a dressing gown, seemingly ready for bed. It's a cue for me to take a shower and eventually exit the washroom, minus a dressing gown, in my Manmade briefs only.

I had thought we'd spend a little more time talking over what to anticipate in the day ahead. But Mae believes we're in need of a respite to relieve mind and body of the stress that threatens to overwhelm us both. 'An interlude,' she terms it, intriguingly.

How thoughtful of her. How stimulating. How quickly it puts the witness statement out of my mind.

She's under the covers, with the lights out, a late evening glow seeping through the curtain. I'm there beside her in the time it takes to dispense with the need for another pour of A Tale of Spices.

Meanwhile she, I discover, has dispensed with the need for sleepwear.

If I had any lingering doubts about compatibility, they vanish in the rush to bare all, to add that dash of extra spice to the interlude.

EIGHT: DAMNABLE

WHAT THE FUCK? Legs over the side of the bed, struggling back into the underwear.

We're deep into sleep when all hell breaks loose beyond the bedroom door. People yelling and swearing like they don't give a rat's ass whose privacy they're invading.

I'm into jeans and sweatshirt and through the door. Mae, in only her dressing gown, not far behind. The ruckus floods the inn.

Down the few stairs barefoot, we run smack into Mort, Bobbie, and Carmel Ann staring at the closed door of Tryphena's room.

'What the hell's going on? Where's Constable O'Rourke?'

None of them knows.

'And Angelo?' Mae throws out.

Tryphena's door is wedged open. Filling the gap is the answer to her question.

'Nobody move!'

'Oh my God!' shrieks Carmel Ann.

The Angelo in the gap has a gun in his hand, which I recognize as Constable O'Rourke's side arm. With whatever sense he's retained, he has refrained from pointing it at anyone.

His scowl makes it clear he might do so at any second. The asshole is sweating. Like he's in a hell of a situation he didn't see coming. 'Nobody move!' he shouts again, and louder.

We're not deaf, you idiot.

He throws open the door. Then retreats inside, leaving us to stare past him. At Constable O'Rourke. Gagged and tied to a chair!

'Oh my sweet Jesus!' wails Carmel Ann.

The constable is bound with what looks like strips of a torn-up bed sheet. Nothing moves except her eyes, electrified and shamelessly pleading.

Almost as alarming is the figure standing at the foot of the bed nearby—a stiffly erect Tryphena Loveless, rumpled bedclothes and a discarded book behind her.

Wearing one-piece, purple fleece pyjamas patterned with what my unbelieving stare now tells me are open books and quotations. The one across her chest being prominent enough to decipher: *Just "one" more chapter.* Frightfully friggin' tacky.

The pyjamaed sight that she is leads me to the conclusion that Angelo came knocking at her door and caught her in mid-sentence. A shouting match, spontaneous or staged, ensued, prompting O'Rourke to come running to investigate And *wham! Bam!* There it is—the aftermath in the chair before our eyes.

Unbelievable. Not that there's any time to let compassion take hold, given Angelo's hand frantically waving her gun.

He herds us along the hall. 'Down the goddamn stairs.'

'No need to swear, Angelo,' says Bobbie. She is strangely unemotional, as if her acting experience has taken hold.

'Shut the fuck up!'

The idiot is desperate to sound like he means business.

Bobbie is not deterred. 'I figured all along you were the one. You got that look about you, like you wouldn't think twice about knocking off someone who rubbed you the wrong way.'

She's missing the mark. To my mind, the fellow's got himself in deeper shit than he ever thought possible, and now he's frantically trying to find a way through it.

Regardless, Bobbie needs to keep her mouth shut. Angelo does have a gun in his hand. The bloody thing could be loaded. It could go off accidently.

'And now you got poor Triffie involved. You blackmailed her, didn't you? You blackmailed her?'

'I said shut the fuck up!'

I quickly put my arm around Bobbie's shoulder and steer her along in the direction the gun is waving.

The stairs he's talking about are behind a high-bolted door at the far end of the kitchen. Where they lead, I have no idea.

'Synard, flick the light switch and open the goddamn door.'

For the well-being of our tormented troop, I'm compliant.

The reason for the childproof bolt quickly becomes clear. The stairs lead narrowly and steeply down into the pit of a cellar.

'Synard, you first. And be fucking quick about it.'

He's overplaying the tough guy. He was bloody insufferable enough as it was.

I steel myself and take the lead. 'Slow everyone . . . One step at a time.'

There's no railing. My bare feet strike the gritty steps.

'Hurry the fuck up, Synard.'

What kind of hellhole is he forcing us into? One that's bloody cold. One with a landing that turns into jeezly gravel.

I hobble painfully aside so the others can get past me. All except Mae, whose bare feet are suffering even more than my own.

A naked light bulb reveals empty, derelict shelving, and in one corner, a cobweb-covered wooden crate stamped *CANADA DRY, The Champagne of Ginger Ales*. Mort hands it to me. I overturn it next to Mae. She sits down.

All the while, asshole is hurling orders for everyone to cough up their smartphones, smartwatches, and anything else smart enough that people could communicate with the outside world. Which means he intends to shut us all in here and bolt the door.

The realization throws the KNOT trio into cold, collective shock. Carmel Ann erupts in tears.

'There's no need, Angelo . . . ' Mort stammers.

'Shut your fucking mouth and do what you're told.'

The idiot fumbles open a drawstring bag while trying to keep a grip on the gun. The bag tells me this shit was planned, that the shouting match with Tryphena was a sham.

'We have no phones. They're back in the room.' I expose my wrists, as does Mae.

He forces me to put my arms in the air and turn around. He's looking for a bulge in a pocket.

Mae's dressing gown has no pockets. 'Let's see inside,' he barks at her.

Without hesitation, Mae stands up, whips open her dressing gown and whips it closed again. 'Satisfied?' she barks back at him and sits down, shivering.

Angelo's speechless. He turns to the other three, all of whom dutifully make deposits into the bag before throwing their hands in the air.

'Now what do we do?' says Bobbie.

'Who gives a shit?' Angelo says. 'Rot, for all I care.'

Your theatrics are falling flat, asshole. By my calculation, after you bolt the door, we'll be here for no more than a few hours before Jeanine shows up for work. The door is not bloody soundproof.

'Synard, up the fucking stairs!'

What now? What the hell? Mae grips my hand.

'Yes, you Synard. Up the fucking stairs!'

Okay, asshole, have it your way. Not before I haul off my sweatshirt and give it to Mae. I kiss her quickly on the cheek.

'You others, good fucking night!'

Utterly pathetic.

Within seconds we're up the stairs and back in the kitchen. He slams the door shut and bolts it. Then switches off the light. A communal scream filters from below.

'Give them a break.' I switch it on again.

He leaves it that way but can't give in without spitting a threat. 'I'll break your fucking neck if I have to.'

'Good luck with that.'

He glares at me snottily.

There's no covering my contempt. 'You want a second murder on your hands? I doubt it.'

'Just shut up, Synard. Don't play the fucking smartass.'

The guy just wants this over and done with, whatever the plan is. He has no intention of killing anyone. The guy's an asshole, but he's not stupid and he's not insane. He's trapped. And he's convinced himself there's a way out of it, whatever the hell that might be.

It looks like I'm one more piece of the plan—part of an insurance policy to somehow get him and Tryphena out of Dildo. A hostage of some kind.

Good luck with that.

The plan, for what it's worth, continues to unfold at breakneck speed. He prods me to my room, rushes me into winter clothes, and adds my cellphone and Mae's to his collection.

He tightens the drawstring and knots it. The bulging bag presents a problem. It's too big and bothersome for him to carry around. Yet, if he just thought about it, he'd realize there's no point in destroying the devices. When Jeanine arrives in the morning, they'll have access to her phone anyway.

In a freakish epiphany, Angelo leads me to the kitchen, where he hauls open the cabinet holding the two bins and promptly drops the bag among the recyclables.

So he did think about it. Not only that, but your typical criminal mind would have sunk the bag into the filth of the garbage bin without thinking twice.

A very telling point. To my mind, Angelo Jones is an accessory to a much bigger plot, one he regrets ever being part of. One that is bound to reveal itself now that I've been seconded to the role of hostage.

If I don't sound shit baked at the thought, it's because, barring an accident with the gun (which, since donning his parka, he's lodged inside one of its pockets), he has no intention of doing me harm. He'll continue to sound as if he would, but in no way would it be any advantage, particularly if he has it in his head that he'll resume the life he led before getting himself into this shit.

As for Tryphena Loveless, during our absence in the cellar, she's managed to change out of her one-piece wonder suit into the nondescript pants and jacket she was wearing when she arrived for the conference. On an emotional level, however, her wardrobe change does her no good whatsoever.

She's nervous as hell, wired beyond anything she's able to handle. More shit for her collaborator, on top of what he's already dealing with.

'Get hold of yourself! You got me into this. And by the fuck, you're going to help get me out.'

Not meant for my ears, but at this point, that's not their concern. What *is* their concern is Constable O'Rourke, who by now has stopped any hopeless fight to release herself and has gone limp in the chair.

Not a boost to either one of them. The fact is, they have assaulted and forcibly detained a police officer. An indictable offence, as they well know. And, I'm tempted to add, it carries a penalty of up to five years behind bars.

But to put it in context, that pales in comparison to a conviction for murder, carried out intentionally or otherwise.

Tryphena exits the room, wheeling not one but two overnight cases—more confirmation that all this was planned. Dickhead pulls the door closed. She locks it.

I have no doubt that the constable will survive just fine. Her RCMP training has toughened her up. She'll be no worse for the wear. Once Jeanine releases the four in the cellar, they'll head straight for the room and cut her free.

The question is, where will I find myself at that exact moment, the same moment someone will be on Jeanine's phone, desperately trying to get through to the RCMP detachment in Harbour Grace?

I have no idea what this pair of erratic schemers has in mind. They have no ready access to a vehicle that's not snowbound. Here we are, trudging through the ice- and snow-covered driveway to the plowed road, Dickhead lugging his own case, me lugging Tryphena's while she frantically checks her phone.

'He just passed New Harbour,' she announces.

'Good fucking timing.'

Some plan is falling into place. Something built to handle the plowed but potentially unsalted back roads of Newfoundland is making its way to us. I stand by, arms folded. With cynical, bated breath.

Sweet fuck.

What slinks into view, as if the devil himself had arrived, is a matte-black, red-accented . . .

Sweet fuck and a half. You're kidding me.

Is that the gold Lamborghini raging-bull crest on its hood?

How about I try not to look thunderstruck a second time. From the lair emerges a perplexing, familiar face. Perplexing because what the hell is the pilot Sven doing here?

'Lamborghini Urus twin-turbo Hyper SUV,' he says to me. 'A bloody beast in the snow.'

Sven fingers a hidden button on the lower inside door panel to activate the tailgate and tosses Tryphena's two cases inside before pressing a second button to close it. He opens a rear door—revealing rich, red-leather upholstery—and ensures that I'm locked inside before opening the passenger door for Jones, and the other rear door for Tryphena.

Sven's been assigned an operation, which he's performing with perfect precision. 'Seat belts,' he snaps.

I'm half expecting the seat belt to operate automatically, sensing my body proportions, then wrapping itself around me and clicking in place. But no, I have to do it all by hand. The tech guys are working on it, I'm sure.

If I sound cynical, it's because I am. A Lamborghini built for snow?

Yet, strapped in a back seat, I can't fault its road handling. The beast is doing it with verve and guts, and although I don't have the full-on, front-seat experience, I'd be lying if I said I was less than impressed.

It's getting us wherever the hell we're going in consummate futuristic style.

We hit Route 80 and turn left, meaning we're backtracking through New Harbour. The Lamborghini is returning to home base.

After more than an hour driving in the dark over a highway that's still treacherous in spots, we make it, thanks to said beast and a pilot who appeared to know exactly what he was doing.

Winterton is dead at four in the morning. The Hyper SUV finds its way through town and comes to a final stop inside a cavernous garage, in a space to the left of a Porsche Carrera and to the right of a vintage Ford Mustang.

The garage door closes behind us. Sven retrieves the overnight cases and leads the way to the interior of the house. I'm second in the line, in front of the still-agitated Jones, who figures there's a need to inform me the gun is in his pocket, ready to be whipped out any time he chooses.

Let's face it, asshole. I'm not going anywhere.

Confirmed by the bark of a Rottweiler that suddenly barges into view as we go past a door and into a cloakroom. The guard dog accepts a chummy pat from Sven but eyes the rest of us with suspicion until someone calls out 'Brutus!' from the next room.

Aptly named, I'm sure. Brutus snaps to attention and retreats, a clear indication that the dog responds unfailingly to commands. No doubt including "Attack!"—code for "Tear the guy who is running away limb from limb."

I soldier on, advancing tentatively inside a high-ceilinged, voluminous foyer.

'Sven, wonderful! I'm sure you could have driven that road with both eyes closed!'

Lonz Littlejohn is nothing if not exuberant is the face of unforeseen complications. He acknowledges Jones with a robust handshake and Tryphena with a broad smile and nod of his head.

'And Sebastian Synard, our guest of honour. So to speak. The person we have to thank for bringing us all together.' Littlejohn's smile narrows to something contemptuous.

Undeserving of a response.

'A washed-up loser who poked his nose where it didn't belong. Synard, you're an absolute fake!' He rears his fist. 'Make us Scilly Cove again!'

The true Littlejohn has exploded into view.

'A loser,' injects Jones, 'who needs to be taught a goddamn lesson.'

As do you, asshole.

Am I scared yet? No. Do I put up with this shit? I have no choice.

What the hell are they going to do? Rough me up, then finish me off? Littlejohn is a wack job, but face it, he'll only do what he thinks he can get away with. Assault and murder with eyewitnesses don't fit the bill. I'm no more than leverage should the cops show up unexpectedly before these goons make a safe getaway. When I'm no longer of any use to them, they'll dump me.

In struts Charmaine to add more weirdness to the scene. She immediately heads for Tryphena and embraces her. The contrast between the two women is bizarre.

Holding Tryphena's hand, Charmaine leads her out of the foyer and into the next room, as if she's needing an escape from the threat of violence. Not that she expected it would come from me.

I turn to Littlejohn and Jones and look each of them squarely in the face. 'I'm playing your game. But lay a hand on me, and I swear to God you'll never utter the word *toponymy* again, except behind iron bars.'

I have the balls when I need them. I follow the women into the next room. Unchallenged.

So this is the place Lonz Littlejohn calls home for three months of the year. It's what showbiz can do for you. Wild success on the silver screen builds you a modernistic mansion overlooking the waters of Trinity Bay, Newfoundland. *The Shed*—a name meant to reflect, one assumes, a longing to recapture the simple, rustic pleasures of his youth.

Thus the floor to ten-foot ceiling sprawl of windows. The cluster of designer sofas—accented with oversized cushions, hand-quilted in seascape patterns. The expansive rug, its wool pile grooved to resemble ocean waves, lying atop what looks to be reclaimed hardwood. Another pseudonostalgic nod to his past.

'Enjoy it while you can, Mr. Synard. I'm afraid we'll soon have to get you on the move again.' Pretentious jerk. 'Who's to say where you'll end up this time.' A pathetic bluff if I ever heard one.

It's no more than a cue for Charmaine to retrieve her Canada Goose parka, together with a bomber version in black for love mate Lonz. Once rigged out, including gloves and MUSCA hats, they steer the less weatherproof of us outside by way of a back door, then down a succession of steps to a cleared boardwalk that leads into an open field. It's snow covered except for a single, circular patch.

On which sits a floodlit helicopter. By its markings, an Airbus H125.

Luminous. Swank. Steely red. Built to get the job done.

In this case, I assume, to get us all to St. John's International Airport. And some of us from there to Florida. But not me. I'm not carrying a passport.

Sven stores the luggage and plants himself in the cockpit, behind the glass-eyed canopy and the radiant instrument panel. He's switched roles, to the one in which his competence is unmistakable. He'll have us to our destination in short order. My guess? In under twenty minutes.

Before taking the co-pilot seat, Lonz assigns the rest of us to one of the four seats fixed tightly across the passenger compartment.

Charmaine takes to the far left, behind Sven and next to the opposite sliding door, making sure it's properly closed and secure before buckling up. A familiar position, it seems. Tryphena nervously slides in next to her, managing finally to fasten her belt.

Dickhead is next. He makes a fruitless effort to get comfortable, not helped by his tonnage or the fight to adjust his seatbelt in order to have access to the gun bulging in his pocket.

I head for the remaining seat.

'Not so fast.' Lonz grabs each of my arms and yanks them behind me.

Now what the fuck?

'Just so you don't get any bright ideas.' He lashes my hands together with what feels like a plastic zip tie.

Jesus.

'Now you're good to go.' The sarcastic bastard forces me aboard and as far back in the seat as the shackle allows.

'Forget the fucking seatbelt,' barks the asshole seated next to me. 'You won't need it where you're going.'

Fuck off with the tough-guy shit. You both do a piss-poor job of it.

Lonz slides the door shut. He manoeuvres himself into the co-pilot seat—not that it's likely he knows anything whatsoever about flying this thing—and shuts his own door. 'Let's get this show on the road.'

Sven, finishing the pre-flight check, gives him a thumbs-up. He sets the rotor blades in motion, their rotation building to the point I can feel the lift. When he sends a surge of power to the blades, we're suddenly in the air, rising quickly over Winterton.

Bent forward in torment, I focus on the view out the window. It does bugger all to ease the rage, but it's a distraction.

The sky is starless, with only a sliver of the moon, and for the first few minutes, the view below is a bucket of darkness. But then a string of lights comes into view, what must be the towns along the western shoreline of Conception Bay. The heaviest cluster is to the south. Carbonear, presumably, and Harbour Grace. I think of Staff Sergeant Larkin zonked out in bed, clueless to the fact the constable he left in Dildo is bound, gagged, and wide awake.

The lights pass under us as a far more intense band makes

itself known in the distance—metro St. John's and the tangle of its satellite towns. I think of Nick, and Gaffer curled up next to him. Lads, there'll be stories told over the finest Scotch I can lay my hands on. I can't wait to set eyes on you both. It'll be early in the morning, maybe even sooner. I expect more theatrics between then and now . . .

The asshole lunges across and grabs the handle of the door next to me.

My brain jolts back to now! 'What the fuck are you doing?'

He hauls open the door, sucking in a blast of freezing air . . . Leaving nothing between me and the black wall of night . . . No seat belt, hands lashed together tight behind my back.

Below me, the open goddamn waters of Conception Bay.

Nothing I can do, nothing but lean as far as I can away from the gaping pit.

'Go for it!' yells Lonz, twisted in his seat.

The fucker next to me grabs my shackled hands and presses them into my back.

Forcing me toward the fucking pit!

The women scream.

Jesus H. Christ!

There's nothing to brace my feet against. I push back as much as I can, but his strength is more than I can resist. He's steadily edging me forward . . .

I shut my eyes until I see stars and tighten my fists until they're rock.

The fucker yanks me back.

I fall across the three of them, banging my head against the other door. He slams the open door shut and, in a sick measure of compensation, elbows me in the nuts.

A deep, fucking groan.

'That'll teach you!' yells Lonz. 'Make us Scilly Cove again!' He pauses to catch his goddamn breath. 'Thank you, Mr. Jones.'

All three of them work to upright me and jostle me back into my seat. I say nothing. Do nothing but suck in air and stare ahead at nothing. I shouldn't have to feel relief, but there's no fucking escaping it.

'Have a look out the window,' says asshole. 'Just think, you'll soon be planting your feet back on home turf. That'll be a relief.'

'Fuck off.'

Lonz erupts in laughter. 'Gotta hand it to you, Synard. You still got balls. We hope.' He laughs even louder.

I stare vacantly ahead, images of Mae swirling through my mind. I pray she's all right. I cling to her until I feel the helicopter starting its descent.

Dickhead lunges across me a second time and hauls open the door. We're at a standstill on solid ground.

'That was a ride you won't forget.'

Sick bastard. I don't respond.

Lonz is standing outside the open door. There to make sure I don't crash to the ground and break my neck. My resentment hits a fever pitch, but I give him his way. The day will come when I will explode on my own terms.

He strong-arms me down to the ground and forces me to one side, to where Sven is standing.

'This is the end of the line, Synard. Consider yourself lucky you're standing upright on land instead of washing ashore. Sven will deal with you. The rest of us have other plans, as you'll find out when it's too late. In the meantime, one final piece of advice.'

'Hurry up, darling,' calls Charmaine. 'Hal's got his clearance from air traffic control.'

So much for secret plans. Lonz offers a final look into his arrogant eyes. He slips the MUSCA hat off Charmaine's head and plants it on mine. 'Don't come looking for me, Synard, or your next helicopter ride will be over the Everglades. If you survive the fall, the alligators will finish the job.'

Pure, certifiable scum. Fucking sleeveen.

He's gone, with the other three. I'm left with Sven.

Just what he intends to do with me is the pivotal question.

To which he offers a partial answer. 'We've got a few hours to kill.'

'Then what?'

'By then you'll be dumped.'

'Alive, I assume.'

'If they wanted you dead, they would have strapped a lead belt around your waist and booted you out the door.'

Once that image is out of my head, there's room for more questions. Like what does he intend to do once I'm dumped? Fly off in the helicopter? That's not going to get him very far before he has to refuel, at which point his whereabouts become obvious.

'You're catching a flight in the morning to Toronto?'

'Enough with the questions, Sebastian. You're alive. Count yourself lucky, and do what you need to do to stay that way.'

Sven I take to be half decent, caught up in shit that he saw no way out of except to do what he was told. Agree to a payoff, catch a flight off the island, and escape into the bowels of the mainland.

Sven checks his watch. It's not yet five. He starts walking and expects me to keep up with him. Obviously, we're not spending hours on the tarmac or back in the helicopter. There's a vehicle somewhere.

'How about cutting this zip tie?'

Suddenly—an eruption of flashing lights outside the perimeter fence.

Sven shows no surprise. 'This is it, Synard. You're on your own.'

He fishes a pocket knife from his pocket and slices through the tie. I rub my wrists and fling the hat on my head to hell.

Several cop cars bolt past an open gate and onto the tarmac, veering to the right of us, in the same direction Lonz and his gang were headed.

Sven is gone, running toward the open gate, leaving me standing in the dark alone.

In the distance, the cop cars have come to a stop, fixed in a circle, headlights trained inward, flooding an aircraft. My one satisfying thought—it's the private jet of scumbag Littlejohn.

I walk tentatively toward it, knowing better than to land myself in the midst of an RCMP armed intervention. I advance to where I have an unobstructed view, yet remain within enough gloom that I'm unlikely to be seen.

Beyond the gloom is an electrifying still life. The fugitive four plus one (the pilot, I assume) are lined up in front of the open door of a small but impressively sleek jet. Its single engine is mounted on the rear fuselage, just to the front of the V-shaped tail. The whole is a metallic crimson red, cut through by an undulating silver stripe.

It's colour coordinated with Lonz in his MUSCA ball cap and Charmaine in her Canada Goose parka. Although with a submachine gun trained in their direction, the couple's status is looking rather limp. As for the other three, *shell-shocked* would be an apt descriptor.

'Really, Officer,' says Lonz. 'Is this necessary?'

Lonz's attempt to downplay the shit in which he now finds himself is not about to meet with the response he's hoping for. Unfortunately for him, it's not his friend, the one-shot actor Larkin, who's at the receiving end of his question.

It's Inspector Ailsa Bowmore. Her comeback is bound to be anything but role play.

'You have the right to remain silent. I suggest you do exactly that.'

'I'm calling my attorney,' Lonz snaps, as if it's an uncompromising rebuttal.

'Go right ahead.'

'He's a legend in Miami,' Lonz declares as he begins to jab in the number.

'But has zero jurisdiction in Canada.'

That stops the idiot in mid-digit.

'St. John's has several excellent criminal lawyers. If you don't have sufficient means to hire one, a court-appointed lawyer can be arranged at your request.'

Bowmore turns her attention to the others. 'That goes for all of you. I suggest you inform the judge of your decision at your first court appearance in the morning. You will need to decide before your bail hearings.'

Bowmore's words add weight to the fact that keeping their mouths shut is the better option for all of them.

The inspector nods to the officers standing by. All five suspects are handcuffed, then led to the back seats of three police vehicles. The St. John's lock-up is about to see a spike in client numbers. It's a weeknight. There should still be lots of space available.

Only when the vehicles are out of sight do I emerge from the gloom and into the glare of the remaining headlights.

'Sebastian! Thank God!'

It would appear that Inspector Bowmore was unsure whether I was dead or alive.

I offer an abbreviated bow and affirming smile. 'Ready, willing, and mostly able.'

'What the hell happened?' The question came from behind me.

I turn to discover Inspector Olsen.

'You sure you're all right?' His concern, which I assume to be genuine, is intense.

'The helicopter ride was a bit of a freak show, but I survived.'

In time I'll get to the details, after the question that's

pounding inside my own head. 'How the hell did you know to show up here?'

'A call came into 911,' Bowmore tells me. 'Anonymous, but whoever it was said people were being held captive at the inn in Dildo, then immediately hung up. It was passed along to the RCMP detachment in Harbour Grace, and when Staff Sergeant Larkin tried contacting the constable assigned to the inn, he couldn't reach her. So he and his officers went straight there and forced their way inside.'

Bowmore is about to tell me what they found, but there's no need. 'Are they all okay?'

'The constable toppled over trying to free herself and struck her head. She's been taken to the hospital in Carbonear to get checked out. As you might expect, the others were somewhat traumatized, but they're fine. They're all desperate to know what happened to you.'

Bowmore is interrupted by another officer who has just emerged from one of the remaining police cars. 'Larkin's on the line. I filled him in, but he's wondering about some guy named Sebastian Synard.'

Bowmore motions for me to join her. Sitting in the front passenger seat of a cop car is a major boost to my morale. My heart rate subsides. My lungs go back to their regular intake of air. I try smiling for the first time in a dog's age.

'Staff Sergeant, I have Sebastian with me on the line. No worse for wear, I'm happy to report. But I'll let him speak for himself.'

Not something I was expecting, but nevertheless, I feel the need to rise to the occasion, knowing that he'll be taking a report on my mental state directly back to Mae.

'It was touch and go there for a while, but I remained positive and in the end they let me go unharmed.'

That's the sanitized version for Mae, for the moment.

In time, when things settle, I see myself putting it another way—it might have been touch and go, but if I could have got my hands on the bastards, I would have wrung their goddamn necks.

It's better if we get off the topic. 'Staff Sergeant, how did you know we were picked up and driven to Winterton?'

'The Lamborghini,' Larkin says. 'Dead giveaway. Once we got to the inn in Dildo, lights to the max, it wasn't long before neighbours showed up, wondering what the heck was going on. Constable Blanchett questioned them in case anyone had seen something around the property earlier in the night. Sure enough, one of them was outside on his deck having a smoke when the Lamborghini pulled up and a bunch of people got aboard. Of course, no one owns a Lamborghini around here except Lonz Littlejohn.'

'And no one else with access to a helicopter.'

Larkin adds, 'Which, when we made a few quick phone calls, was confirmed to have been sighted flying out of Winterton.'

Got to hand it to the Mounties. Once they get the tip, they're dead-on target to get their man. In this case, two men and two women. Arrested for assaulting a police officer, unlawful confinement, conspiracy to cause bodily harm, and—in due course—homicide. Not to mention threatening to dump an individual from a helicopter into the icy waters of Conception Bay, where—had he survived the fall—he would have struggled in the throes of hypothermia and drowned.

Thankfully, a question from Inspector Bowmore clears my head of that particular scenario. 'Staff Sergeant, any idea of who the informer might be?'

'We've reviewed the 911 tape several times. He was on the line for only a few seconds. Not much to go on. We could detect a slight accent.'

'Sven,' I say.

When I think about it, there is no one else it could be. He was the only one who had anything to gain from spilling his guts, which would be to offset the charge of being an accessory to the crimes.

'Sven?' says Larkin.

'The helicopter pilot.'

'You mean the guy who came running off the tarmac?' says Bowmore.

'That's the guy.'

'The RNC were on standby in the parking lot and nabbed him.'

Got to hand it to the Constab. According to Bowmore, Olsen had wind something was up with me at roughly the same time that Sven blew the whistle on what was going on in the inn in Dildo. I need to know how. I exit the cop car and head in Olsen's direction.

'Frederick, my man. What's up?' Overtly calm and back in control. I never want Olsen to think he's gained the upper hand.

'Sebastian, I'm good. Just how the hell did you get yourself into this mess?'

'Better yet, how the hell did you know I was in it in the first place?'

We've become very good at maintaining a competitive spirit. It gives our relationship a certain equilibrium.

'Nick,' Olsen tells me. 'He called to say he'd been trying to text you and got no response. And when he phoned, there was no answer. The same thing when he tried reaching Mae.'

'He knew something was up.'

'Actually, the way he put it, there was a good chance you were in deep shit.'

Nick has this habit of overreacting.

But okay, in this case—not a particularly bad thing. Olsen gets in touch with Bowmore, and there you have it.

Boom, I'm on the radar of both police forces.

'Consider yourself lucky,' says Olsen. 'I had visions of you with a bullet in the head.'

Really, Olsen? How good of you to share.

'Actually,' I say, 'if you think about it, it makes no sense that the fellow who stole the constable's gun would have used it on me. He's in enough shit as it is.'

Olsen bites his tongue, rather noticeably. Out of sympathy for what I've been through is my guess. I might as well have the satisfaction of seeing him chomp down even harder.

'For the same reason,' I continue, 'it would have made no sense for the fellow to have pushed those few extra millimetres when he hauled the helicopter door open, ready to catapult me into the North Atlantic.'

'Fuck.'

Precisely. 'Just between me and you.'

We leave it at that.

NINE: GAYSIDE

ALL'S WELL THAT ends well? Not exactly.

I am alive. That's a very big plus.

The reception I received when I showed up at home just after dawn was gut-wrenching, beyond anything I was prepared for.

'Dad. Holy God.' The rest was tears and a hug so hard it left me a paternal basket case. To say nothing of Gaffer jumping at me until I sank to his level, where he practically devoured me with his licking.

We eventually settled into interaction that vaguely resembled what we had before I set off on the freaking escapade. And I did manage to get some sleep, broken though it was by repeated visions of a seemingly endless fall.

Mae drove straight from Dildo as soon as Bowmore gave her consent to leave, which wasn't long after the investigators arrived, knowing as she did how desperate Mae was to see me.

Mae got to my house by mid-morning. She collapsed in my arms, the emotion of it all finally finding release.

'I'm so sorry,' I said. 'I should never have convinced you to get involved.'

'Don't be crazy,' she said through tears. 'We got through this. We had each other.'

So something positive did come out of this bedlam.

I made the decision not to tell Mae or Nick about what went on in the helicopter. There might come a time when I would. But for now, it's for me to deal with.

In the meantime, there's the practical pieces to set back in place. Mae came back without any of our things because the investigators weren't finished with the room. There's that, and I have to get the rental off the parking lot of the Dildo brewery and back into the hands of the Turo owner. This means driving there in my car with Nick, collecting the Sprinter, and driving it back to town, Nick following behind me in the car.

Not something I'm looking forward to doing, but if I can scrounge another couple of hours of actual sleep, we should be good to go by one o'clock, when Nick gets back from the gym.

I'm out cold on the sofa when the doorbell rings. It stirs Gaffer from his guardian perch in the crook of my legs. He jumps to the floor and barks his way to the door. I follow drowsily behind.

It's Heather. I probably look like death warmed over, but I'm more than happy to see her. She tried reaching me by phone, but that was obviously a lost cause.

'I thought I'd take a chance you were back home.'

'Barely.' I use a hand to flatten my unruly hair as I lead her inside to the living room.

There's a story to be told—which takes a while since she knows all the characters—only interrupted sporadically by "Good God, Sebastian" or variations thereof.

When it comes time for her to explain why she needed to connect with me, it might have proved anticlimactic. Far from it.

'I've been making some additional inquiries. About Carmel Ann this time. From the moment she got in touch with me about covering the conference, I sensed there was something off about her, something that didn't add up. Her name for one. As you know, *Buttery* is uncommon to begin with, but pairing it with *Carmel* seemed contrived, rather bizarre, given it's so close to *caramel*. Something a parent would think twice about before naming their child. No matter how sweet she might have looked.'

'I once worked with a guy named Richard Head. He was forever cursing his thoughtless parents.'

'Exactly.' Heather pauses. 'Guess what? *Buttery* is not her birth name.'

'You're kidding.'

'Remember you told me she retired from the Mississauga Wellness Spa? I contacted the administrative office, pretending I had sat next to a Carmel Ann Buttery on a plane and was wanting to reconnect with her. They knew no one by that name. They did, however, know someone named Carmel Ann who retired several months ago, whose full name was—would you believe it?—Carmel Ann Freake.'

Jesus, she's a Freake! 'You got to be kidding. Originally from Newfoundland?'

'And too close to the description I gave them not to be her.'

'Don't tell me she's related to Bobbie Freake.'

'Sisters. Mentioned in the obituaries of both parents.'

'No!'

'Which also means she's an aunt to Lonz Littlejohn.'

I can only shake my head.

'Let me get this straight. Carmel Ann grew up in Baytona—or what was Gayside—while Bobbie grew up in St. Chads, the former Damnable?'

'Probably not. Bobbie may have lived there as an adult. Or, never lived there at all. In other words, made that part up to expand the range of KNOT.'

I need time to get my head around all this. There is no time.

'There's more.'

Give me strength.

'I dug deeper into the family tree of Tryphena Loveless.'

'Don't tell me . . . '

'Her mother's maiden name.'

'Her mother was a friggin' Freake?'

'Who married a Loveless.'

'And you're telling me Triffie's related to the two sisters?'

'Possibly. I'm still working on that.'

'Good God, Heather, you're amazing.'

She smiles modestly, but rather playfully. But then, just when I'm about to return the smile . . . Was that look in her eye a hint of something more?

It hits me that her fact-finding mission might not be for the sake of the investigation alone.

My psyche stiffens. Flirtation is not what I want or need at this stage of the game.

'We make a great team,' she comments.

I hesitate. 'That we do.' I suddenly realize I haven't mentioned Mae to Heather.

Have I not done so unconsciously? Or purposely? Regardless, why am I not mentioning Mae to her now?

Because it would be signalling that I suspect she's coming on to me, and what if she's not? Then that would make it flat-out embarrassing. Besides which, I don't want to be putting a wet blanket on our relationship, considering all she's done for the investigation so far, with the prospect there's more yet to come.

Make sense? I try.

'Where do I take it from here, that's the question,' I say. Unquestionably referring to the investigation.

'If the three women are related,' Heather says, 'then did

they, for whatever reason, join forces on a scheme to poison Richard Martin? To my mind, that's the first question.'

'I was getting to that.'

'And if they did, how do Lonz Littlejohn and Angelo Jones fit into the picture?' she adds.

'That, too.'

I must sound like I don't know whether I'm coming or going. All because of a look she gave me, or didn't give me.

Now the look she's sending my way is one of sympathy. A look that seems to be bordering on pity. 'I realize you're still in recovery from your near-death experience.'

A brutal way of putting it.

It hits me that I told Heather about the "near-death experience," something I kept from Nick and Mae.

Fuck. My head is in spin cycle.

If there was ever a time to get my shit together, this would be it.

'I gotta get to Dildo, the sooner the better. To confront the Freake sisters.'

'Sebastian, are you sure that's such a good idea, considering your headspace at the moment? Isn't it best left in the hands of the RCMP?'

'I know for a fact that my headspace is quite capable of dealing with my near-death experience. My partner, Mae, has no problem whatsoever with my headspace.'

Rather snappy, unfortunately.

Heather is taken aback. Understandably. 'I think I better go,' she says. 'I have things to do.'

She stands up. I do the same. The awkwardness won't be easily overcome. But there's no point in not trying.

'Sorry if I sounded impatient.'

'Resentful, you mean.'

'You could say that.'

'I did say that.'

Gaffer whines, tactlessly.

Heather heads to the door.

'Sorry I was being a pain in the ass.' It's the best I can do.

It's no help. She opens the door.

'Heather, please, I'm serious. What you've done is awesome. It's thrown a whole new light on the investigation. Where it will lead, I have no idea at this point, but, wherever it is, we'll have you to thank.'

'By "we" I assume you mean the RCMP. Like I said, they need to be in on this.'

I don't confirm it. 'My son, Nick . . . The two of us are driving to Dildo together.'

'Sebastian, don't take any chances, please.' Sympathy alone this time.

'I won't.'

'One close encounter was enough.' Then she's out the door, closing it behind her.

There's one good thing. "Close encounter" is sounding a whole lot better than "near-death experience."

Nick is hardly in the house when I hit him with the plans, and by one o'clock, the two of us, plus dog who is unwilling to let me out of his sight, strike the Outer Ring Road heading west.

PI and son share a thermos of strong coffee. We make do with tiresome granola bars. Both of which are beside the point.

We're tearing straight toward a decisive turning point in the investigation. Picking up the Sprinter has been abruptly shifted to second place, replaced by an encounter with the soon-to-be dumbstruck Freake sisters and a squad of RCMP officers.

It takes all my willpower to keep close to the speed limit.

'What if they deny any relationship to Tryphena Loveless?' Nick says as we sprint past Paddy's Pond, the city well behind us.

'That's where it's bound to get interesting. That's where they're going to have to cough up answers to some basic questions. Including, why has your sisterly relationship been under wraps until now?' I thump the steering wheel for emphasis. 'And, did you two happen to fake your upset about being sent to the cellar, when all along you were in cahoots with the yahoos who wrenched me away before your very eyes?' Another thump.

'Including,' says Nick, 'are you in fact now shit baked because the yahoos now in the lock-up just might rat on you? And, wouldn't it better for you to come clean, because the cops might just go easier on you if you point the finger at who exactly came up with the scheme to neutralize Richard Martin?'

'Very good point.' One I actually hadn't thought of, as yet.

Nick always has been a fast learner. It blows me away how quick he was at getting a fix on the criminal mind.

'I like that—*neutralize*.'

The word has a measured quality. The lad's got what it takes.

'To be honest, Nick, I've never been comfortable with "murder." I have doubts that killing him was the intention. They wanted Richard Martin to look weak and out of the picture so he wouldn't dissuade anyone from voting to change the name back to Scilly Cove.'

'So why invite Richard to the conference in the first place?' Nick says. 'Why not just make it a rally for the MUSCA crowd?'

That I have thought about. 'KNOT wanted to come across as being in favour of free speech. They wanted to make it look like they were impartial by giving the other side a voice.'

'When in fact, in all the sessions, they were doing what they could to suppress it.'

'Exactly.'

'Then they could say, "You had your chance. It's not our fault you screwed it up."'

Father and son in investigative sync. Does my heart good, just when I need it most.

By the time we turn off the Trans-Canada, whipping along the last few kilometres into Dildo, we're psyched, ready for action. With sun all day and the temperature up, the snow has taken a beating. As we turn into the inn's plowed premises, I notice that Carmel Ann's colourful Ford Fiesta has emerged from the snowdrifts and is no longer on the parking lot, which leads me to conclude that the RCMP have impounded it.

But neither do I see any police vehicles. In fact, the only vehicle on the lot belongs, if my memory serves me right, to Jeanine. Have the Mounties come and gone?

The guest entrance is locked. I ring the buzzer and wait impatiently.

Jeanine opens the door. 'Mr. Synard, you're all right, thank God. I heard what happened. Come in, come in.' She looks like she wants to give me a hug, but she can see I'm not keen. I introduce Nick to divert her attention.

'You're here to collect your things. When the police had finished with your room, I took them out and set them safely aside. I hope you don't mind. I needed to clean the room for the next guests.'

'There's still an officer here, I assume.'

'No, everyone's gone, the RCMP included.'

'By everyone, you mean Carmel Ann and Bobbie? And Mort?'

'They were still upset after all that's happened, but they were anxious to get away, as you can understand. As soon as the police had finished with them, they packed up and took off.'

'In Carmel Ann's car? All three of them?'

'I assume so. They said something about going to Pitcher's for lunch. I assume Mort was going to stay there until someone drove in from Winterton to pick him up.'

'How long ago?'

'Maybe an hour and a half, give or take. I was busy with Staff Sergeant Larkin when they left. He had more questions about how I discovered the bag of cellphones.'

'Which included mine and Mae's.'

'I was about to put out the recyclables when I noticed the bag was unusually heavy.'

I know the rest. I just want the two phones and our stuff. 'We're in a rush. We have to pick up the van.'

'They called from the brewery wondering if I had any idea who it belonged to. It's blocking the exit to their parking lot.'

Jeanine is left addled by our scramble to get away. She was counting on a first-hand account of all I had gone through.

'You sure you don't want a cup of tea and a molasses bun?' she asks as she hands us the phones.

'Next time.' We're out the door without looking back.

Harsh, I know. I do wave to her as I back up and drive away.

The change of plans has threatened to throw me off balance. Not likely.

It takes less time to get to the brewery than it does to make up my mind about what we do next. 'They got rid of Mort. Now they're back on the highway. We take the van and chase down the buggers.'

'Shouldn't that be left to the police?' Nick says.

'First, Larkin's back in Harbour Grace, and Bowmore and her crew are probably in St. John's by now. We're here, that much closer to the action. Second, Larkin would have to buy into what Heather has uncovered. More time. Third, if and when Larkin did show up, I'd have to convince him where I think they're headed. *More* time. We need to get to the Freake sisters while we have the chance.'

'They assume the cops are finished with them. They think they're in the clear, for now.'

'They know they have time to make a getaway.'

'So they fly out of St. John's or Gander,' says Nick.

'Not so fast. Think about it. They're not frantic. They'll want to go home and pack up the car with all the stuff they'll need to take with them, considering they might never be coming back.'

'So the ferry to Nova Scotia.'

'Exactly. Their one choice is Port aux Basques. It's a nine- or ten-hour drive, but that doesn't bother them because they have a planned stop along the way.'

'Checking the ferry schedule . . .' Nick's phone coughs it up. 'There's a sailing tonight, but they'd never make it in time. After that, eleven forty-five tomorrow morning.'

'So they drive so far, spend the night, then leave early in the morning to drive the rest of the way.'

'And as we both know,' Nick says, 'that overnight stop will be . . . '

'Where else but . . . '

In unison, 'Baytona!'

Gaffer barks his loud approval. He's pumped. Almost as much as I am. The brain came through the near-fucking-death experience with flying colours. 'We show up in Baytona, track down the Freake sisters, and put them through the investigative wringer!'

And with that, I turn into the entrance to the brewery's parking lot. 'I'll grab the Sprinter. You take the car and park it at the inn. Tell Jeanine we'll be back for it ASAP. She won't mind. Tell her we'll phone ahead so she can put on the kettle and dig out the molasses buns.'

With most of the snow melted, the Sprinter revealed itself, skewed across the parking-lot exit. My desperation to get on the road is all the excuse I need not to venture inside to apologize.

By the time I settle Gaffer in the van, scrape the remainder of the melting sludge from its windshield, and manoeuvre deftly out the exit, Nick has parked the car and is waiting at the end of the inn's driveway. As he climbs aboard, I wave back at Jeanine, who's waving eagerly from one of the dining-room windows. I'll be sure to get in touch with her at least an hour before our return, meaning we'll be met with a fresh batch of molasses buns straight from the oven.

Fifteen minutes later, we've hit the Trans-Canada at Whitbourne. I pump gas while Nick scours the Circle K for sandwiches and Gatorade. We're back on the highway in record time, heading west and deep into Google Maps.

'Next stop—Baytona,' says Nick. 'Which should take us three hours and twenty-six minutes.'

'So roughly six-thirty.'

'Considering how you're chomping at the bit, that's a conservative estimate.' He grins. 'Just remember, we don't want to arrive before they do.'

'Smartass. All we're aiming for is to get there in daylight. We wouldn't want a showdown in the dark.'

Nick is back at his phone. 'According to Time and Date dot-com, the sun will set at 8:23 p.m. That's set in stone no matter how fast you drive.'

'May I suggest you place that last comment where the sun don't shine.'

Leaves the kid straining for a comeback.

I'd revel in it longer but have other things on my mind. 'That gives us two hours leeway.'

'*Leeway* meaning pee breaks and supper.'

'*Leeway* meaning a side trip.'

'You're joking,' Nick says. 'Like to where?'

'Like to Fair Haven, the former Famish Gut.'

'Really. *Pourquoi*?'

Switching to another language supposedly emphasizes his bewilderment. The semester he spent in Saint-Pierre studying French has had varied results.

'How do you say *covering all the bases* in French?' I ask.

'Baseball isn't part of the culture. *C'est dommage.*'

'In that case, let me put it to you in plain English. As we know, Fair Haven is where Tryphena Loveless has been living since her breakup with Richard Martin. The turnoff to Fair Haven is not far from here. I figure we take a dash down on the chance the Freake sisters showed up there. Because if they did, then it could confirm the link between them and Tryphena.'

'Have we really got time?' he says.

Google does its job. Route 203—13.7 km.

'Like I figured, there and back in less than half an hour.'

Nick shakes his head. 'Plus the time it'll take to find the house, then find someone who just happened to have noticed two women showing up there within the past hour.'

'It's outport Newfoundland. No one stays anonymous for long.'

Nick knows better than to think I'm going to be dissuaded.

'You're in charge,' he says. Facetiously, I'm sure, given that I detect a perverse satisfaction in the fact the Route 203 isn't quite as user-friendly as anticipated. Navigating potholes is not in the Sprinter's job description. Neither is being stuck behind a school bus.

And once we actually reach Fair Haven, there's an unwelcome discovery. It's not the compact, snug little seaside community I had envisioned but is, in fact, strung out around a deep channel of Placentia Bay, presumably the *gut* in Famish Gut. Most of the houses are generously separated one from another with some, to judge by the sideroads, in among the trees and out of sight.

Nick can barely contain himself, especially given that I can't seem to locate a convenience store, my investigative go-to stop when I show up in an outport and need to find out the home of someone I know but, as I tell the store clerk, don't quite remember the exact location.

'Seems you struck out this time,' says Nick.

Absolutely not, as it turns out.

Plan B is to stop the first person I see on the road. In this case, there is only one choice, a middle-aged woman in a classic Adidas track suit, moving briskly, arms swinging. I assume she would normally move to the gravel shoulder when a vehicle happens by. In this case, because of the buildup of snow left when the road was plowed, the vehicle moves to avoid her.

We've passed her once already, and having backtracked after failing to find a convenience store, I bring the Sprinter to a halt and roll down my window. I wait for her to stop and chat as I know she will do. Again, it being outport Newfoundland.

'Excuse me. Sorry to interrupt your jog. I'm looking for a friend of mine, Tryphena Loveless. I was hoping you might know where her house is located.'

'You mean Trif?'

'Yes.' I smile, with a quick glance to catch Nick's eye. 'That would be her.'

'Or Triffie. Some people call her Triffie.'

'Yes, indeed they do.'

'Used to be married to that two-timing Dickie Martin?' the woman says.

I'm getting more info than I bargained for. And maybe even more if I play my cards right.

'Yes, that's her,' I say. 'I knew Dickie. I knew him as Richard.'

'Growing up here, he was always called Dickie.'

I had no idea Richard/Dickie grew up in Fair Haven.

'He'll always be Dickie to us. Or, as hes grandfather used to call him, little Dickie bird from Famish Gut.'

It's no wonder he ended up in toponymy.

'So they grew up together, Tryphena and Richard?'

'Childhood sweethearts, Trif and Dickie. They went off to

university together, and before you knew it, they tied the knot.'

I try to keep the chat going while the going is good. 'I was surprised he would cheat on poor Trif.'

'You heard what happened to him?' she says.

'Not really.'

'Overdosed. In a way.'

'You're kidding.'

'That's what I heard,' she says. 'Threw away hes EpiPen and set off hes allergy on purpose. Dead before they got him to the hospital.'

'My God, how awful.'

'Awful is right. Awful to see what it all come to for poor Trif, after starting off so young and in love. Never know what life's got up its sleeve, now do you?'

Tell me about it.

'You were asking about her house.'

We did get sidetracked. 'Yes, could you give us directions?'

'No point. Sold. About a month ago.'

'Another curveball,' mutters Nick, who has been mostly dumbstruck since the woman's first words.

'Trif ended up back in Fair Haven after she and Dickie broke up, but no one was surprised she didn't last. As it was, she spent part of the winter in Florida. From what I heard, she met someone down there. Of course that's only rumours.'

'Of course.'

We're pressed for time, and the jogger's store of information has veered to speculation. In any case, she starts jogging on the spot, a clear indication that she intends to resume her workout.

'One last question,' I say. 'I understand Trif was related to the Freakes, on her mother's side. The last time I saw her, she was with two sisters—Carmel Ann and Bobbie Freake. Do you know if Trif was a relative, or just a friend? I wasn't sure.'

'Carm and Boo-Boo. Of course they're related. Cousins. Growing up, they'd come to visit in the summer. The three of them—thick as thieves. Carm and Boo-Boo was bridesmaids at Trif's wedding.'

The icing on the cake, so to speak.

She's off then, back in motion. I wave out the window as we move on, and make for the highway.

We hit the intersection with the Trans-Canada and head west, having logged another twenty-two minutes. Not surprisingly, Nick is quick with the calculations. 'Fifty-six minutes total.'

'Well worth it. Not what we anticipated, but a gold mine nonetheless. Things are adding up, Nick my man.'

'A freakin' stroke of luck.'

'I think of it as calculated luck.'

'Gaffer and I have to hand it to you. You manipulated your way through that pretty good.'

Gaffer yelps. I'll mark that down as an endorsement.

I glance at Nick. 'Thanks, son. I try.'

'Nobody expects the Spanish Inquisition.'

We both chuckle. Gaffer only smirks.

Our shared addiction to Monty Python aside, the encounter with the Fair Haven jogger lined up a few more ducks.

'I'm thinking, given the ribbing Richard endured growing up, any suggestion of changing Fair Haven back to Famish Gut was particularly galling to him. He would be out to nip that in the bud.'

'And his ex-wife would only be proposing it to get back at him,' says Nick. 'Agreed? But what I don't understand is, wasn't that obvious to him, her being right there at the conference?'

'Puzzled me too until I thought more about it. I don't once remember seeing both of them in the same room. She avoided him. Spent her time in the kitchen and out of his sight. He likely didn't even know she was a member of KNOT.'

'So Tryphena and her cousins gang up to do a number on Richard? Really?' Nick says. 'They organized the conference for revenge? KNOT is all a hoax? I'm not sure I buy that. Seems like too elaborate a hoax. Too many things could go wrong.'

'And did.'

'But then how does Lonz Littlejohn come into play?'

'The jogger did say Tryphena met someone in Florida,' I tell him.

'They met by chance? Not likely.'

'You're forgetting Bobbie and Carmel Ann are his aunts. They could easily have set it up.'

'So they get to talking,' says Nick, 'and the more they talk, the more Lonz sees that, working with Tryphena, there might be a way to get Winterton changed back to Scilly Cove? Even so, it's a huge scam, with a lot of moving parts.'

'Lonz Littlejohn makes movies,' I remind him. 'It probably looked to him like small potatoes. He's very used to manipulating the truth.'

'So he starts this MUSCA campaign to give it momentum.'

'Then arranges his Stagehead Scilly Cove as the venue for the climactic event of the conference—Richard Martin's speech.'

'And the rest is history,' says Nick.

'Not quite the history they intended. Their intention was, like you said, to neutralize Richard, not to have him die in an ambulance on the way to the hospital.'

A half-hour on the highway, and we reach Goobies. Hardly the time to be making a stop, but we have no choice. First, to do our business using the facilities of the tourist-information centre, and second, to let Gaffer do his. The statue at Goobies is, without doubt, his all-time favourite urinary-deposit spot—the rear right hoof of that iconic life-size tourist attraction, Morris the Moose.

Missions accomplished, we're back on the road in less than no time.

'Next stop—Damnable.'

'You're not serious,' says Nick.

'I need a definitive answer as to whether Bobbie Freake ever lived in Damnable/St. Chads. So yes, I am serious. And, yes, go ahead, do the math.'

Nick allows Google to do it for him, of course. 'Via Route 310, 23 km, roughly twenty-three minutes.'

'Perfect.'

'Down and back, with who knows how long to get the definitive answer—at the very least, an hour.'

'That's being pessimistic,' I say.

'Sixty minutes which, when added to the time from there to Baytona, plus at least one pee break, brings us in at roughly ten minutes past sunset.'

'The twilight zone.'

'You said we need to get there in daylight.'

'Twilight is daylight, roughly speaking. Besides which, we need to factor in how much time I'll gain, as the opportunity arises, by edging past the speed limit.'

'While all the time praying we don't run into construction.'

'Too early in the year, pal. Still frost in the ground.'

We could be sparring all day. However, Nick knows me, and he knows when to hang up the gloves.

He moves on to something where he does have a choice. He opens the bag of sandwiches.

'Chicken, roast beef, or knuckle?' he says. 'What's your preference?'

It takes me a while. 'Smartass.'

'Not among the choices, I'm afraid. I'd say go for the chicken. It should suit you just fine.'

'Bugger.'

'Yes! You know you got him good when his only recourse is vulgarity.'

'My recourse is Damnable.'

We'll call it a draw. Which I'll admit gets harder to do as time goes on. You raise them to take a joke and, before you know it, the joke's on you.

But, as luck and smart planning have it, Damnable sees me flying high yet again.

'Who calls a place Damnable?' says a skeptical Nick, as we turn off the Trans-Canada and head toward St. Chads. It's one of seven communities on the Eastport Peninsula. The peninsula's sandy beaches are familiar territory to both of us, having vacationed on them numerous times when Nick was a kid, pre-divorce. But St. Chads we've never ventured to before.

'As I understand it, the origin of the name is up for debate. Apparently, navigating its coastline in a sailing ship can be a bit of a challenge. A disgruntled settler came up with Damnable Bay and Damnable Island.'

'So why miss out on the opportunity to christen your hometown Damnable?' says Nick.

'Who would resist? However, that story has its detractors.'

'Damn.'

'That said, the fallback involves pirates.'

'Yes. Pirates always add a certain cachet when it comes to naming a place.'

'So a pirate ship was hiding out in the harbour to escape the British,' I tell him.

'The cocky British, in a man o' war, no doubt. And the pirates yelled "Frigate," that's "Damnable!"'

'Close. One of the pirates struck the ship's bell by accident . . . '

'By accident?' says Nick. 'It's already sounding dubious.'

'By accident, and it echoed far out in the bay, alerting the

British, at which point all the other pirates yelled, "Damn the bell!" Which, on subsequent yells, morphed into "Damnable."'

'Doesn't strike home with me. I vote for the first option. A swearing settler trumps a pirate who swears by accident every time.'

I can't top that. I can only smile broadly.

St. Chads (more than a century ago renamed at the urging of a Reverend Wilson, an uninspired local minister) looks to be home to no more than a few dozen people. I suspect if it did have a convenience store with a helpful clerk, it was in the distant past.

As we loop around the community, there's no action. Homebodies abound. I'm sure, in time, some unsuspecting person will emerge from one of the houses and make his or her way to the one and only road, but we don't have that kind of time.

I pivot to another rural investigative strategy, one I've perfected over the years. I decide on what looks to be the house with the most promise of yielding results, and go knocking. In this case, it's a solid two-storey, garden nicely maintained, with a bird feeder and a broad veranda with two Adirondack chairs, both looking to have been recently painted.

In due course, my usual friendly, rhythmic knock brings an elderly man to the door. He looks pleased to see me despite having no idea who I am. So far, so good.

'You must be Willie's son.' He holds out his hand. I shake it regardless. 'Willie said you might come by if you had time. Come in. Come in.'

I'm very sorry to have to disappoint him. I suspect he doesn't see many people. But I can be the best of company for several minutes. I explain what brings me to St. Chads. He's quick to tell me he's never known anyone by the name of Roberta Freake.

'Some people would know her as Bobbie. Or maybe even Boo-Boo.'

'Don't ring a bell, neither one of 'em. And I've lived here all me life.'

That clinches it.

He turns aside and calls to someone nearby. 'Mabel, ever hear of a woman be the name of Freake livin' in St. Chads?' (Except he pronounces it *Sin Chads*. The Rev. Wilson would not be pleased.)

The answer is a weak but audible *no*. Twice clinched.

'Thank you very much, sir. You have been very helpful.'

'Sorry to disappoint you. To be honest, I wouldn't mind knowing a Boo-Boo Freake. Sounds like she'd have a bit of life left in her.'

With that, our chat has definitely run its course. 'Have a good day. I'm sure Willie's son will be along shortly.' Strategy complete.

Nick and I are back on the Trans-Canada in fifty-five minutes from when we turned onto Route 310 and Nick activated the stopwatch on his phone. Five minutes cut off the twilight zone. I try not to be smug.

Distance remaining to Baytona? 'That would be 154 kilometres,' according to Nick. 'Gander is roughly halfway.'

Gander is invariably on the radar whenever I'm driving into central Newfoundland. It's the town in which I was rooted in my youth. Beyond that, in the early decades of transatlantic aviation, the necessity of flights stopping in Gander to refuel prompted the label Crossroads of the World. And now, following 9/11 and the *Come From Away* phenomenon, Gander has regained its star power.

It is also the place where my sister resides. Unfortunately—or fortunately, whichever way you look at it—we have no time to stop and visit. Family dynamics are better left unmentioned, as Nick well knows. I *will* say the relationship has improved from what it once was. A positive that gives rise to the possibility of stopping during the course of the return trip, should the timing work in its favour.

When we do reach Gander, having consumed a considerable amount of Gatorade, we need a pit stop. Gaffer finds a suitable location behind Tim Hortons. Once he's completed his round of sniffing and returns to the Sprinter, Nick and I proceed inside, for the washrooms and sour-cream glazed donuts, a favourite of all three of us.

With Gaffer still sighing contentedly, we're back in motion, firmly focused on the next and final stop.

'Carmel Ann was a woman who thought she was a loner
But she knew it couldn't last.
Carmel Ann left her home in Gayside, now Baytona
For some Mississauga grass.'

Nick's singing cracks me up when I least expect it.

We've been clowning around with this road-trip game for years. Sometimes all we do is substitute a place name in a song with the name of the Newfoundland outport we're approaching. Other times, Nick likes to milk it for all it's worth.

'Not bad. The rhythm is a bit off.'

He ignores me. His voice goes higher.

'Rush back, rush back / Rush back to where you once were wronged . . .'

I join in.

'Rush back, rush back / Rush back to where you once were wronged . . .'

Nick goes solo. *'Rush back, Carmel Ann.'*

As we turn off the Trans-Canada at Notre Dame Junction, the mood takes a U-turn. Had we the time, Route 340, known as the Road to the Isles, would take us along a splendid chain of islands, culminating in the town of Twillingate, the Iceberg

Capital of the World.

Mid-May is generally when the monoliths start showing up, having been swept along the coastline from Greenland. But with luck, there might be a few early bergs as a primer for the tourist trade.

Icebergs, however, are not on our minds. What we'll face when we strike Baytona very definitely is.

'Dad, you sure you're prepared for this? There's still time to call in the cops. The Lewisporte detachment is like twenty minutes from Baytona.'

We've been through this before. Cold feet is the last thing we need.

'Local cops would have no idea what's going on. They'd have to be convinced to have a showdown with the Freake sisters, which would mean the rigmarole of contacting Bowmore in St. John's to get the background and determine whether I'm legit. We don't have that kind of time.'

Nick hesitates. 'I hate to state the obvious.'

I sense what's coming. I'm not going to like it.

'Perhaps you should have gone to straight to Inspector Bowmore yourself,' he says. 'You could have convinced her to do something. She trusts you.'

'That's debatable.'

Is that enough of an answer? It's all I'm about to offer.

I manage to avoid sounding frustrated. 'We leave it to the cops, and by the time they get their act together the Freake sisters will be long gone.'

Nick won't argue the point, but neither is he conceding it. 'Aren't you even considering they may be armed?'

'Not for a second.' Absolutely not. 'They're two half-decent women who got themselves into a situation over which they lost control. It went hopelessly wrong and turned to murder.'

'To which they are suddenly accomplices.'

'Exactly,' I say. 'They figured by being locked up in the cellar with the rest, they looked totally innocent to the cops. They're simply scared shitless of being found out and figure the best thing to do is get themselves as far away as possible from the whole situation.'

'Okay, say you're right. Aren't the bunch in the lock-up just going to paint the sisters as the ones who came up with the scheme to get rid of Richard?'

'Possibly. Littlejohn is sure to have a courtroom thick with high-powered lawyers. Who knows what dirt they'll have up their sleeves?'

There it stands. Nick has cooled down somewhat. He might have more questions but chooses to keep them to himself. In any case, he'll soon have the answers. And in full-on twilight. The sun has barely gone down.

The sign for the turnoff to Baytona is just ahead. And coming into view before it is the perfect opening act—Baytona's own North Atlantic gas bar and Kwik-Way Convenience Store. In short order, I'm inside at the counter, paying for a couple of ice-cream bars, my go-to purchase when I'm really there to hit up the store clerk for information.

'A friend of mine asked me to drop off a package to Carmel Ann Buttery. You wouldn't happen to know where she lives?'

'You means Carm Freake. I know she changed her name, but to me she'll always be Carm Freake. Since she came back home, she's been living with her sister, Boo.'

'I see.' It's all coming together.

'Just past the Anglican church. Purple bungalow. You can't miss it. Only Boo would paint her house purple.'

I wonder if she has any yard art.

We're back in the Sprinter, eyes peeled for the Anglican church. Between bites of the ice-cream bars, the decision is made on just how to approach Bobbie Freake's purple bungalow.

'If I park in the driveway, they'll recognize the Sprinter right away.'

'That is, if anyone happens to be in the house.'

'Enough, Nick. It's time to get in the game.'

He holds up his hands. 'Okay, okay.'

'We'll pull into the church parking lot and approach the house on foot.'

'Got ya.'

A bit too enthusiastic to be convincing. I let it pass.

The Anglican Church of St. John the Evangelist welcomes us, as revealed by our headlights striking the sign attached to the handrail of its front steps.

I park in the rear of the empty parking lot. We exit the Sprinter. It's roughly 8:38. We're still heavy into twilight. I'm ready to tackle whatever lies ahead. Whether Nick is remains a question.

What lies immediately ahead is Carmel Ann's Fiesta, parked in the driveway of sister Boo's bungalow. All right! The stunning green-and-purple combo demands a smug look in Nick's direction.

There are lights on, including one over the front door. The driveway, however, leads to an unlit side door.

'The less direct light, the better.'

'The lesser of two evils.'

I dig him in the ribs.

He groans. 'I was being serious.'

'Sure you were.'

'I am now.' He produces a tightened fist. Ignoring the doorbell, he thumps the door.

'Hell, Nick, you'll scare the bejesus out of them.'

Two seconds later, we're flooded in light from a pair of fixtures, one on either side of the door.

The sheer curtain covering the window that fills the upper

half of the door is drawn back, and the face of the resident Freake sister appears.

The curtain immediately drops back in place. The door doesn't open. No detectable movement inside.

We look at each other. Now what happens?

We wait. And wait, keeping one eye on the green machine in the driveway to be sure they're not about to attempt a getaway through the front door.

This time it's me who thumps the door, simultaneously ringing the doorbell.

Again we wait. Finally the door is opened, tentatively, revealing Carmel Ann and Bobbie Freake, stiffly erect, unsmiling. Holding hands.

The sight, against my will, strikes at my heart. I feel more certain than ever that they have been snared by a scheme not of their own making.

Carmel Ann asks the inevitable question. 'What are you doing here?'

'This is my son, Nick. We're here to help you through what happened. You know and I know that both of you have a lot of explaining to do. The RCMP will soon know it too.' I'm playing it nice, but direct and to the point. 'I think we should come inside.'

Their hands slowly disengage. They quietly stand back. We enter the house and I gently close the door behind us.

The sisters lead us inside, not to a living room—as I expected—but through an open door to a small sitting room, furnished with an aqua sectional sofa extending along two walls. Mounted in the corner opposite is a flat-screen TV with a screen saver of Monet's water lilies. There's a small, circular oak table bearing a china plate of what look to be Purity Ginger Snaps, and three partially filled teacups, also china, also with a pattern of Monet water lilies. Impressionistic to say the least.

'Have a seat,' offers Carmel Ann.

My mind is on the tea cups. 'You have company?'

The sisters sit together on the other sectional. 'You could say that,' says Carmel Ann.

Into the room steps the third person. And there you have him.

Mortimer Auberon Coveyduck.

Decidedly uncomfortable, fighting for all he's worth not to show it.

How much exactly is he worth? In particular to the Freake sisters, who seem to be intent on gauging my reaction to the sight of the man standing before us, in a characterless white shirt and tie and a navy blue cardigan. But with the notable addition of a pouch clipped to his belt, from which hangs what looks to be an oversized meat tenderizer. Heavy duty, polished, stainless steel. Wide, back-to-back hammer heads, one flat, one deeply serrated, at the end of a lanky, black-grip handle.

Good God. Not that I think Mort would ever have use for one, given, I take it, he recently arrived at the house in the role of someone other than chef.

'About to pound a few steaks are you, Mort?'

He doesn't crack a smile. Rather, his seriousness intensifies, performance though it is.

Boo-Boo Freake takes the stage. 'He could pound your head into the wall if we need to.'

I don't know whether to laugh or deliver a fiery rebuttal. I try something more calculated. 'Roberta Freake, we stopped in your Damnable on the way here. Nobody's ever heard of you. I assure you, the police will be interested in what you are attempting to hide with your boldfaced lie.'

'Not that you'll ever have the opportunity to tell them,' says the adjoining sister, with concentrated effort.

Another one desperate to act tough. For what reason? To

intimidate us into going back to where we came from? Surely to God they don't think we're going to fall for this hard-ass routine.

'Thank you, Carmel Ann. I was wondering when you were going to join in. What other pearls are you about to dispense?'

Nick jabs me with his elbow.

I turn to find the meat mallet in Mort's right hand. He pivots it up and down, determined to look villainish.

I have to admit it's a fearsome piece of steel he's got there. In the hands of someone deranged, it could do serious damage. Mort, as everyone in the room knows full well, is far from deranged.

'You're getting carried away, Mort. You've been watching too many horror movies.'

'Obviously, Sebastian, you haven't seen *Death by Sirloin*,' injects Carmel Ann.

Nick looks at me, eyes wide, meaning *what*? That he has seen it?

'It's the same murder weapon,' he mutters.

'That's right, Nick,' says Bobbie. 'In fact it's the *exact* same meat mallet. A Dalstrong War Hammer! The props guys let me keep it as a souvenir.'

She jumps up from her seat and snatches it out of Mort's hand. 'Sit the hell down, Mort. You've haven't got the hang of it.'

Before our eyes, she transforms herself into what I assume is some vile character in *Death by Sirloin*. By the look of it, the one who committed the murder(s).

Dear God, what are we witnessing? It was impossible for them to be naturally tough, so they had to resort to acting the parts from some third-rate horror movie?

'Okay, you two, I've had enough,' shouts Bobbie. 'If you want out of this kitchen alive, then smarten the fuck up!'

'There she is!' exclaims Carmel Ann. 'Winner of the best supporting actress at the Die Laughing Horror-Comedy Film Festival!'

Bobbie takes a slight bow before resuming her role. 'I don't think either one of you want your brains turned to mush. Do you?!'

I refuse to play along. 'Not necessarily.'

Bobbie slams the meat tenderizer onto the plate of ginger snaps, pulverizing both the cookies and the plate, and doing serious damage to the table.

'Oh, shit!' she says. Only confirming her conduct was out of character.

'Ah, Boo,' moans Carmel Ann. 'Look what you've gone and done. I know how much you loved that plate . . . and our dear mother's table.'

Boo is not deterred. She jumps back in. 'By the hell, you'll not show up in my kitchen thinking you're going to demote me to sous-chef! I'll have you drawn and quartered!'

'Is this where the meat tenderizer comes into play?' I ask snidely.

Nick is not so cynical. The theatrics are getting to him. 'Watch it, Dad. She's going off the rails.'

I don't buy it for a second. It's all an act. 'Put that thing down, Roberta! Get real. You two sisters—yes, the jig is up—are in serious shit. Running away from it will only make it worse when the cops catch up with you, and believe me, they will catch up with you, whether it's when you get off the ferry in Nova Scotia, or driving the back roads to wherever the hell you might be headed.

'Florida,' blurts out Mort.

'You meathead!' yells Bobbie. She swings the tenderizer in his direction.

'I told you it was ridiculous,' counters Mort, if rather weakly.

'What chance would we have to get past border security?'

'Zero,' I point out.

The tenderizer is redirected at me. 'Nobody asked you, numbnuts!' Bobbie straightens herself and closes her eyes for a couple of seconds, as if reclaiming her movie role. Her grip tightens on the War Hammer.

'Sous-chefs, prepare the sirloin! It's time to put these jokers to the test!'

She's still at it. What's it going to take to bring her down to earth? In the meantime, Mort and Carmel Ann exit the room. For where—the actual kitchen?

Nick, I regret to admit, is still falling prey to her antics. 'The movie was called *Death by Sirloin* for good reason,' he intones.

'Exactly!' Bobbie declares. 'And that part, you'll be sorry to hear, wasn't particularly funny.'

Enough already. In fact, more than enough!

She raises her meat tenderizer, swinging it slowly back and forth, ever nearer to us. 'The sirloin is about to find its way onto the Japanese teppanyaki cast iron grill . . . '

'Damn it all, Bobbie. Shut up!'

She sucks in a deep breath, to reinvigorate her venom.

'Listen to me! Your Florida plan is defunct. Lonz Littlejohn is in the slammer in St. John's. So are Charmaine, Angelo, and your Fair Haven cousin Tryphena!'

Is this something she already knows? Was she told of it this morning by the cops in Dildo? Most likely.

Nevertheless, the War Hammer takes a jerking descent to her side.

'Bobbie, listen to me.' Quieter now. 'It makes no sense for you and your kitchen pals to be going anywhere except to the RCMP to explain what part you all played in this fiasco.'

Bobbie Freake sinks to the sofa, the tenderizer limp beside her.

The deflation is a remarkable sight. Her performance armour has been penetrated. Truth prevailed. I reiterate the sordid details of the helicopter ride and the scene on the tarmac in St. John's.

She sighs, 'Lonz is out of the picture. His movie-making days are over.'

'For now, at the very least. He'll have other things on his mind until it's clear who exactly is responsible for the death of Richard Martin.'

And it's true. This may spell a sudden end for the horror-comedy career of one Boo-Boo Freake.

'It wasn't me. I didn't kill him,' she exclaims, her voice reaching the same pitch as in her performance piece.

Except it's far from an act. 'Carmel Ann, Mort,' she calls. 'Forget the sirloin.'

The kitchen crew are back in the room in short order. They had to be standing just outside.

Bobbie is building up the strength to explain the change of plan. 'There's no need,' Carmel Ann tells her. 'We overheard it all.'

'I, for one, am not surprised,' says Mort.

Bobbie looks at him despondently. 'You're as deep in shit as we are, bucko.'

'You two got me into it,' says Mort.

'You were up Lonz's ass,' says Bobbie. 'It didn't take much persuading.'

Nick and I are wide-eared, speechless bystanders.

'It wasn't me who stole his EpiPen,' Mort says.

'You sure as hell was the one who knew it was in the pocket of his winter coat,' Carmel Ann reminds him. At which point she breaks down crying.

'I blame it all on Triffie,' counters Mort. 'If she wasn't so resentful . . . '

Bobbie warns him. 'You leave Triffie out of this. If there's anyone to blame, it's Lonz. It was his idea. He got the powder.'

'You mean Angelo got it for him,' says Carmel Ann through her tears.

'I hope the cops throw the book at the both of them,' declares Mort, as if it somehow lets him off the hook.

There's a lull. Dare I ask a question? I need to do it before their inhibitions kick in again.

'Why would Lonz do such a thing?'

'He's all about power, about getting his own way,' says Carmel Ann. 'When he offered to fund KNOT, we jumped at the chance. We wanted to have a conference, but we had no money. He offered to underwrite it all. With conditions attached. Like who would be the guest speakers, where the second day of the conference would be held.'

'What we would be serving for the meal at the closing banquet,' says Bobbie.

'Of course, only after he talked it over with Triffie,' says Mort.

I sense resignation. Of the three of them, actress Bobbie was the one who spent time in Florida and had direct contact with nephew Lonz Littlejohn. Therefore, wasn't it also likely that Bobbie was the one who introduced cousin Triffie to Lonz?

I'd say more than likely. At this point I don't raise the question. I don't want to chance interrupting the steady stream of details.

Youthful, inexperienced Nick, on the other hand, is all too quick to take that chance. 'Were you aware that Lonz was going to show up in person on the day of the banquet?' At least he keeps his voice low and emotionless.

'No!' declares Carmel Ann. It's triggered a response she can't hold back. 'That's when everything went off the rails! Before the banquet, Lonz came up to the two of us and, out of the blue, asked if we knew Richard was allergic to shellfish. Of course we knew. Of course we had arranged for an alternate meal. Then he asked if either of us knew whether he had an EpiPen and where he kept it, just in case anything went wrong.'

'We assumed he had one,' says Bobbie, 'but neither of us had any idea where he kept it. And we weren't about to ask Richard, in case it gave him the impression he might have to use it.'

'Even at the time, we thought it was an odd conversation,' adds Carmel Ann. She and her sister turn and sink their eyes into Mort.

'Lonz asked me the same thing,' says Mort sheepishly.

'And?' prods Bobbie.

'I helped people to hang up their coats when they came in the hall. That was all. I just happened to notice Richard double-check one of the pockets, and I saw a red case with a white cross on it. That was all.'

'Did you describe the coat to Lonz?' asks Nick.

Otherwise how would he know which one to choose? Good point, Nick. In fact, very good point.

'I did not,' says Mort decisively.

Nick shows no surprise. 'Therefore, it would have been Angelo who took the case. He had seen Richard in his winter coat and knew exactly the type and colour of coat to look for.'

Well done, Nick. Youthful, investigative brain getting sharper by the minute. The apple doesn't fall far from the tree.

'I wouldn't trust Angelo as far as I could throw him,' says Bobbie.

'He came with an agenda,' adds Carmel Ann. 'No two ways about it.'

'You mean he was out to discredit Richard before the two even met?' says Nick, who appears to be on something of a roll.

'When Angelo spoke that first night of the conference, it

was like he was goading Richard.' A supporting observation on my part.

'To put it mildly,' says Carmel Ann. 'At the time, I was pissed off he did that. There was no need to be anything but professional and civil. Now I see he did it because he had nothing to lose. He knew, when the time came for Richard to refute anything Angelo might say, the fellow would be in the throes of an allergic reaction, unable to speak.'

'He just didn't count on him being dead,' Mort says, naively sarcastic.

'And you all figure Lonz put him up to it?' I ask, pressing my luck, probing for more.

'Of course he did,' insists Bobbie. 'Not only did Lonz pay his conference fee, no doubt he slipped him a pile of cash under the table for supplying the shellfish powder.'

'The two of them were in on it from the start,' says Carmel Ann. 'When Triffie entered the picture, they couldn't believe their good luck. They convinced her to do their dirty work in the kitchen.'

'Which you three knew nothing about?'

'Not until it was too late. Not until we got barred in the cellar and Triffie took off with Angelo.'

It's all been set in their minds. For our benefit? A rosy portrait of the three of them as innocent bystanders.

Really? I don't think so.

Is it in any way logical that Tryphena was in on the plot to trigger Richard's allergy, yet she kept it a secret from her two cousins? And if they had nothing to hide, what was the reason for the hullabaloo when Nick and I showed up here a half-hour ago?

'I'm curious,' says Nick, looking at Mort, 'why you came here and didn't go back home to Winterton when the police were finished with you at the inn in Dildo.'

That, too. Why, Mort, if you weren't on the run because you knew your pal Lonz could blow your cover anytime?

Mort shrugs, in a way that makes it look as if he has no problem with Nick's question. Yet he doesn't attempt an answer. Instead he nods to Bobbie.

She's thinking, no doubt desperately.

'Carm and Mort and I have formed a partnership.'

A what? A partnership. Partner-shit is more like it.

'We're here now to work on a business plan. We intend to market a line of T-shirts using the lost place names of Newfoundland. The profits will fund KNOT now that Lonz is no longer backing us.'

This takes the friggin' cake! How gullible, in the name of God, do they think we are?

'As the saying goes, "When you reach the end of your rope, tie a KNOT and hang on,"' she adds.

I snap back, 'How about, give someone enough rope and they'll bloody well hang themselves!'

Enough is too much. Cut the crap. Fess up. Spill your friggin' guts.

'The fact is, innocent or not, you three have a ton of explaining to do. Either you stay here and have the cops show up, mad as hell because you weren't forthcoming with the details when they spoke to you this morning, or you do a U-turn and head into St. John's and directly to RCMP Headquarters for a face-to-face with Inspector Bowmore. The choice is yours. I'll tell you this . . . Cops are a lot more hospitable when someone turns up to volunteer information than when they have to track them down and force it out of them.'

If not dumbstruck, they are at least speechless. If they had any common sense left, they would have known this was coming.

The three of them look at each other, no one willing to be the first to respond. Carmel Ann, presumably because she is the president of KNOT, is looking like her nerves are particularly raw.

'Speaking for myself,' she says finally, 'I'm gutted.'

That's it?

'So am I,' says Bobbie.

'That goes for me, too,' adds Mort.

I lose it! 'So you're friggin' gutted. You're so friggin' gutted you want to serve time in the slammer for failing to come clean. What the hell does it take to get through to you guys!?'

'We're scared, Sebastian,' blurts out Carmel Ann, and erupts into tears, again.

And so they should be. I suck down a deep breath. 'You might be scared, but for God's sake be sensible.'

To her credit, Carmel Ann finds a way past the snivelling. 'We never broke the law in our lives.'

'We got caught up.'

You could put it that way, Bobbie, if you haven't got the backbone to be direct.

'We couldn't see the forest for the trees,' says Mort.

That goes for you, too, Mort.

'Tomorrow morning, bright and early, you follow us into St. John's. I'll call ahead to Inspector Bowmore and tell her to expect you. I'll lead you directly to the parking lot of RCMP Headquarters. You'll get out of your car, walk up to the door together, go inside past security. You'll follow the directions to the inspector's office. You'll stand there and knock—ready, willing, and able to face the music.'

While they take time to search each other's eyes, I turn to Nick. I'm sure he's thinking what I'm thinking. You can lead a horse to water . . .

Each in their way seems to reach a conclusion.

Bobbie clears her throat. 'We guess so.'

Combined with slight nods from the other two.

That's as affirmative as they get.

Nick and I spend the night on the adjoining sections of the sofa in Baytona. Gaffer, retrieved from the van, sleeps strategically in the corner between us. We were exhausted, and despite the whirlwind of a day, manage to get some sleep.

Carmel Ann had kindly extended the invitation to stay the night and provided quilts and blankets. I say kindly because she seemed to be wanting to compensate us for the reception we received when we showed up at the house.

Despite her inclination to resort to tears, I still think of her as the most level-headed of the lot. I'll defer final judgement until after the session with Inspector Bowmore.

I no longer have doubts that it will take place. When the others weren't looking, Carmel Ann assured me it would. As I said, level-headed. She's resigned herself to swallowing the pill, no matter the consequences.

Bowmore will be fair with them, as long as they're upfront with her. I texted her when I woke up this morning. It's hard to gauge how she reacted to the sketch of the story I delivered. I would say surprised but restrained. No doubt she's pissed that I took things into my own hands. But she knows me. She knows that's par for the course. Whatever, she had to be grateful when I revealed there's more to the suspect trio than she thought when she sent them on their merry way from the inn in Dildo. (I didn't use quite that turn of phrase.)

We fold the bedclothes and pile them neatly on the sofa before preparing ourselves for what the outside world has to offer.

I'm feeling chipper as we enter the kitchen. 'Good morning, folks.'

They're sitting silently at a table, facing coffee and, as I see from the box and empty packets, Quaker High Fibre Raisins & Spice.

Carmel Ann holds up the box. 'You're welcome to it.'

'We're good. I think we might have some leftover sandwiches in the van.' Stale though they would be.

'I'd have a coffee.' Nick has a slight bounce in his voice, in his own way adding a boost to the morning.

'Love a coffee,' I add. As Nick has sensed, we do want to be encouraging of the change in their demeanour, despite the fact neither one of us is keen on instant oatmeal.

We sit around the table, an odd lot of adversaries who've hammered out an agreement despite the meat tenderizer of last night. I'm feeling chipper because it could have turned out much worse. You keep your sense of humour and your faith that when all is said and done, common sense will return.

'You don't give up easily, Sebastian.'

Coming from Bobbie, I take that as a compliment.

'Thank you. And I have to say you're a swell actress.'

'I thought the War Hammer would have brought you to your knees, but you persisted.'

'I had confidence you'd do the right thing.'

That brings a smile, though, I suspect, not an entirely sincere one. She's thinking about an acting career on the skids.

Mort has yet to speak. He's still running hot and cold. He's had time to reflect on his return to Winterton and the close ties to Lonz that will undoubtedly draw scrutiny from his friends and neighbours. His standing within the community is bound to come up short.

Carmel Ann remains the most steadfast of the lot. 'We all have our ups and downs,' she says, returning the oatmeal box to the cupboard and clearing the table of the now-empty bowls. She quickly washes them in the sink and sets them on a drying rack. 'Drink up, folks. We don't want to be late for Inspector Bowmore.'

I see the collection of bags and overnight cases near the side door. Once she gives the word, it'll be load-and-go. Thank you, Carmel Ann.

Potentially three cheers, in fact. One for each of them. Except I know better than to be counting chickens. It'll take roughly five hours to get to St. John's. A lot can go wrong during five hours of sitting together discussing just what they're going to be saying to the inspector once they reach her office. Including changing their minds about whether they should even be making the trip.

'Nick and I have a proposal.'

Carmel Ann, again taking the lead, gives us her full attention. She puts aside the last cup and wipes her hands on a dish-towel. 'We're all ears.'

'You've all had a very stressful couple of days. How about you relax in comfort while I drive you all into St. John's? The Sprinter invites you aboard.'

'Tempting as it may be, Sebastian,' she says, after checking out the surprised expressions of the other two, 'there's a big problem. How will we get around once we're in St. John's? And what about getting back home?'

Presuming they won't be staying put in police detention. 'Nick's your man. He'll be more than happy to follow behind us in your vehicle.'

A longer pause while she continues to mull it over.

Mort breaks the silence. 'I wouldn't say no. To be honest, it's no fun being cramped up in the back seat of a Fiesta.'

'Excuse me, Mort,' declares Bobbie. 'Just because I'm shorter than average doesn't mean I should be confined to the back seat. It's not my fault I suffer from claustrophobia.'

'Nobody suggested where you should sit,' he says. 'I was merely pointing out that my knees have nowhere to go.'

'Considering I just cut you off at the knees . . . '

Only Bobbie thinks it's worth a smile.

Still, their exchange does prod Carmel Ann in the right direction. 'The massage therapist in me knows only too well that cramped knees could lead to back problems. We definitely wouldn't want that.'

Well, that's fortuitous.

The upshot of it all is that the gang of four plus dog are out the door, to the church parking lot, and aboard the Sprinter within several minutes.

In another half-hour, I'm turning left onto the Trans-Canada and heading east, Fiesta driver Nick following dutifully behind. I'm thrilled, while Gaffer delights at having companions to share his extensive living quarters.

The KNOT trio, for their part, turn suddenly silent. I venture to guess they have been running on adrenalin for so long their bodies have given up in protest. By the time we approach Gander, they are each in turn dead to the world.

So inconsiderate, muses Gaffer, his head resting on his outstretched paws. Not only that, pal, there'll be no return stop in Gander for another sour-cream glazed as you no doubt anticipate.

The patient dog is forced to wait out a muted hour until we reach Clarenville. As is Nick, who I'm sure must be gut-foundered by now. I pull the Sprinter into the Tim Hortons parking lot, the only one awake, in need of coffee and nourishment (beyond one bite of a stale sandwich) to ensure I stay that way for the remainder of the drive. Turning sideways in the seat, I clap my hands exuberantly three times.

'Wakey-wakey! Rise and shine.'

Not what they wished for, but why should they have the luxury of sleep while I get to navigate the Trans-Canada, listening to yet more depressing news about the rise in inflation.

The lunch break is definitely in order. In choosing ubiquitous Tim's, I made what I thought would be the least contentious choice. At this point, still not fully awake, my passengers don't need to be facing surprises on a menu.

Nick leading the way, they drag themselves inside while I direct Gaffer beyond the parking lot to what he feels is a location acceptable enough to do his business. Just as we return, Nick emerges with the canine's donut of choice. Gaffer settles in the van, satisfied that it's been a fair exchange for services rendered.

Tim Hortons has the added benefit of being conducive to mundane conversation. We tackle the chili, wraps, and BLTs while I listen to their complaints about the weather and the pros and cons of heat pumps.

Then, out of the blue, Carmel Ann says, 'I might as well give up my dream of opening a wellness spa in Baytona or Gayside or whatever the frig you want to call it. When the time comes, I might as well go back to Mississauga and be done with it.'

'My acting days are long gone,' says Bobbie. 'Once the producer gets wind of this, they'll sure as hell be recasting the role of the sausage-factory worker.'

'I'm thinking I'll have to give up writing a history of Scilly Cove,' says Mort, 'and move into St. John's and live with my sister and her silly cats, as much as she'll hate it. As much as I'll hate it.'

How heart-wrenching is that. I set aside my half-eaten BBQ chicken wrap. I've lost my appetite.

If they were involved in the death of Richard Martin, they must be held accountable. That goes without saying. Yet it rattles me to hear them cast aside their lifelong passions.

'You're good people. You strayed.'

Uttered against my better judgement. It is yet to be revealed exactly how good these people are—or, for that matter, how far they strayed. Or what the consequences might be. Yet they can't be abandoning their deepest passions. Not at this stage of the game.

'Giving yourselves over to the law is a perfect first step. Be upfront and honest with Bowmore, and see what comes of it. It might reach the point where you'll need to pool your resources and hire a lawyer. But please, you can't despair and abandon hope.'

Of the three, Carmel Ann is looking at me most intently. 'You're going to make me cry, Sebastian.'

'Please.'

Mercifully, she keeps her emotions in check.

I've said my piece. I focus on my coffee, eventually giving in to the need for another bite of the wrap.

No one else speaks. Their appetites, too, are winding down. Except for Nick, of course, who manages to pack away a 3 Meat Hat-Trick Flatbread Pizza, garlic bread, and a double-chocolate donut, and still look hungry.

We return to the vehicles, but although the KNOT trio is firmly awake for the couple of hours remaining in the trip, I hear little in the way of conversation. What does reach my ears are terms of endearment directed at Gaffer. In my experience, being a dog lover is a strong indication of being a decent human being. So perhaps I should trust my instincts.

TEN: FAIR HAVEN

THERE'S A LOT to be said for sitting solo at home, after midnight. In a subdued pool of lamplight in the favourite comfy chair, son and dog upstairs, sound asleep.

The only sound the pour of Glenmorangie into a Glencairn glass.

The only other companion a yet-unopened book. It had been pushed through the mail slot of my empty house sometime earlier today. Not by any postal worker. It arrived without packaging or address. Just the bare paperback.

I say *bare* also because it has a rather provocative cover—an image of a half-naked woman from behind, her bare breasts partially reflected in an oval mirror. Her face somewhat hidden by her raised right arm, the hand resting against the intricate bun of hair woven tightly just above the nape of her neck.

'*Un chignon*,' Nick told me. Which I assumed was a more chic name for the hairstyle.

But the woman is not French, she's Italian. As is the writer Elena Ferrante, the author of *My Brilliant Friend*, which I have heard of but haven't read.

The Days of Abandonment, the book in my hand, I know nothing about.

'Doesn't look like your type of book,' Nick had said. To judge by the cover alone, that's true.

A bigger question is, who owned the book and thought I should have it. And how did the book find its way through the mail slot?

I finally open it to the first chapter and begin to read.

One April afternoon, right after lunch, my husband announced that he wanted to leave me.

Its opening line is all the clue I need. This has to be the book Tryphena had promised to give me.

It's not a surprise she knew my address. As a member of the executive, she would have seen my contract, where the address was clearly stated. She might even have known there was no one in the house. Any one of the other three could have been in touch with her from Baytona.

For that matter, she could have arranged for someone else to drop the book through the mail slot. A cab driver even.

In any case, it is here, in my hands, and Tryphena, for all intents and purposes, is out of my life. At least in the short term.

Late yesterday afternoon, in the course of the bail hearing, she was released—as was Angelo—pending trial for unlawful confinement and pending further investigation into the death of Richard Martin.

Lonz and Charmaine were also released, also pending further investigation. They are to report to the police when requested, at which point formal charges could be laid. Including, I assume, threatening to dump me in Conception Bay.

In the meantime, no one is to travel beyond their residential address in Newfoundland. Their passports have been confiscated.

I don't know where Tryphena is living, but I assume the others are in Winterton, possibly including Angelo, as guests of foiled ringleader Lonz. No doubt their relationship has taken a big hit, so perhaps Angelo has struck out on his own in some short-term rental. In any case, nobody's heading south of the Canadian border anytime soon.

The outcome of the bail hearing came my way via Frederick. The outcome of Inspector Bowmore's face-to-face with the KNOT trio comes directly from the inspector herself.

'On the surface, at least, they were forthcoming,' she tells me over the phone. 'They willingly revealed that they suspected something was up when Littlejohn started asking them questions about the Richard Martin's allergy to shellfish. They were, however, adamant they had nothing whatsoever to do with what they called "Lonz's scheme."'

Which is no more than what they coughed up to me in Baytona. 'And they told you that Littlejohn also questioned them about the EpiPen?'

'Yes,' she says. 'And Mort admitted he told Littlejohn he saw what he thought might be the case for the EpiPen in the victim's winter coat in the closet.'

'The three of them confessed they thought Littlejohn was up to no good even at that point but did nothing about it. Don't you find that odd? And doesn't that make them culpable?'

'Odd—you could say that. As for being party to the offence, that would depend on whether someone knowingly understood that a person was about to commit a crime. If they admitted they witnessed someone stealing the victim's EpiPen, for example, or saw someone sprinkling on food what they knew was powder that could cause an allergic reaction. They denied any such knowledge.'

Inspector Bowmore is sounding like her professional self. I add, 'In other words, they're laying the blame squarely on Lonz Littlejohn and Angelo Jones.'

'It appears so.' There's a pause.

The longer it continues, the more charged it gets. Bowmore's holding back. She's conflicted, the result of our long-standing relationship.

'Ailsa, I am the person who put you on to this.'

'I realize that.'

'Except for me, these guys might be on the lam in Nova Scotia.'

'Possibly.'

'Are you remembering that, less than forty-eight hours ago, I was dangling from a helicopter over Conception Bay?'

If that doesn't do it, nothing will.

'Carmel Ann said something . . . '

I wait her out.

'She said she doesn't know what to believe anymore. That after Lonz Littlejohn came into the picture, she couldn't tell truth from conspiracy. She said he tried to convince KNOT that Richard Martin was standing in the way of its goals, that Martin needed to be replaced by someone who was on their side. Littlejohn said he had influence in government circles. That it could happen.'

It's plenty to set the brain cells in motion. What path they take is another question.

'What do you think, Inspector? Is *she* being truthful? If she is, then it adds a chunk of evidence in the case against Littlejohn. But who's to say it's not all a scheme on Carmel Ann's part to divert blame from the three of them and add it to the case against Littlejohn? And what if he pleads not guilty, which I fully expect he will do. And in a trial, lays the blame right back on Carmel Ann and the other two? For sure, he'll be hiring a slew of high-powered lawyers.'

'He already has,' she says.

The conversation has reached a standstill. We've come to the same sobering conclusion.

'When all is said and done, it's for a jury to decide just who is responsible for the death of Richard Martin.'

'Beyond a reasonable doubt,' I note.

As we both know, money and lawyers can work that clause to great advantage.

In the meantime, the investigation continues. Who's to say what other path it will take.

'In the meantime, the three of them are free to go?'

'We had no basis on which to detain them. They can be called in at any time for further questioning. They were served notice they're not to leave the province.'

There we have it. For now.

'Thank you, Inspector. I appreciate this.'

'Thank God, Sebastian, you're alive.'

Very nice. That personalized ring of sincerity is a definite boost to the soul.

'Oh, by the way, Staff Sergeant Larkin asked me to remind you, to use his exact words, "to get his damn butt in gear and email his witness statement ASAP." He's lost patience.'

'Oh, right.'

As right as another pour of Glenmorangie's A Tale of Spices.

For one thing, it's a very moreish dram. For another, it helps me handle the Ferrante tale of marriage upheaval. Of course, the book triggers recollection of my own marital breakup, although the protagonist's despair was nothing Samantha felt, that's for sure. And as for the husband in the book who split for a younger woman, that wasn't me.

Nick is right, it's not a book I would search out. But Tryphena gave it to me for a reason, and I stick with it, leaving me to think that, in *Days of Abandonment*, she found something in common with her own sad state.

It's a rough read. The buildup of resentment sends the abandoned wife over the edge. She lashes out, violently at times, not only at the husband but at innocent people around her, including her own young children. It's a cruel narrative of mental volatility, until she finally regains the strength to move beyond her bitterness.

Did Tryphena take from the story motivation for harming the husband who had abandoned her? I would have thought, like the protagonist, she learned to accept a situation she couldn't change, no matter how unfair she knew it to be.

Did Lonz Littlejoin take advantage of her resentment and lead her past her common sense? Did MUSCA sap her willpower to the point she lost sight of the truth?

Time and the courts will tell.

'You're in severe need of some downtime,' Mae says to me the following evening.

I'm back from Dildo, having made one last trip with the Sprinter and Nick to pick up my car. (Jeanine's molasses buns were everything I anticipated, and more.)

I'm now at Mae's place, devouring a burger and parm fries from Andersons, where she stopped on the way home from work. She knows how much I love what Andersons delivers when it puts local beef, cheddar, maple-bacon jam, and chipotle aioli between two halves of a brioche bun. It delivers awesome.

'Clear your head of anything whatsoever to do with KNOT,' she continues, beside me at her kitchen table. 'Think of it as a once-in-a-lifetime experience that's never going to repeat itself.'

'That's not the half of it.' A verbal shrug.

If I sound skeptical, it's because I am.

'Let your mind move on to other things. Take a break from the stress.'

'I will.' I'm smiling. 'I keep having this sinking feeling.'

Her hand presses against mine. 'At least you haven't lost your sense of humour.'

'Actually, in retrospect, dangling from a helicopter over Conception Bay has its comedic elements.'

'Laughter is known to be a great stress reducer.'

'That and sex.'

'Really? As I said, you haven't lost your sense of humour.'

'That's not the half of it.'